OUT OF THIS WORLD

CHRIS WOODING

SCHOLASTIC PRESS · NEW YORK

Library of Congress Cataloging-in-Publication Data available

ISBN 978-1-338-28934-3

10 9 8 7 6 5 4 3 2 1   20 21 22 23 24

Printed in the U.S.A.   23

First edition, August 2020

Book design by Christopher Stengel

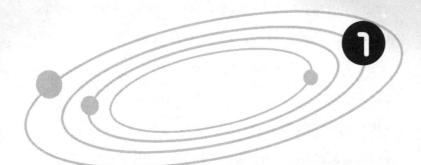

"Anyone home?"

Jack peered through the open door, down the unfamiliar hallway of his house. There were no paintings, no mirrors, no furniture there. Only neat white walls.

"Mom? Dad?"

The silence made him nervous. They were always waiting when he got home from school, and their cars were still in the driveway. He shouldered his backpack and stepped inside, leaving the summer heat behind. The chill of the air-conditioning raised goose bumps on his bare arms.

"Hello?"

No reply. He poked his head through a doorway into a crisply organized study, where Dad did whatever he did when he was working from home. Something to do with finance or business or stocks and shares. He'd tried to explain it once, but Jack had glazed over.

He wasn't there now.

Jack retreated and looked through another door, expecting to find the living room. He found a dining room instead, with a long rectangular table and brand-new chairs. For a few moments he thought the house had somehow rearranged itself while he was out, but then he remembered. It was their *last* house that had the living room opposite the study. Or maybe it was the one before that? These rentals all looked the same, especially since his parents never decorated. And they moved around a *lot*.

He crept up the hallway, listening. Maybe they were out back in the yard. Maybe they were taking a nap. Maybe they had headphones on, listening to music.

None of that seemed likely. They both had

uncannily good hearing, they never napped, and as far as he knew, they never listened to music, either.

There was a muffled noise from the kitchen at the end of the hall, where the door stood open.

"Mom?" he said quietly. Now ice was creeping up his spine. That wasn't the sound of his mom cooking in the kitchen. It was the sound of someone trying not to be heard.

Jack's heart began to thump in his chest. His eyes were fixed on the doorway. Through it, he could see the kitchen counter and the windows beyond that looked out to the backyard.

He should go into the kitchen, find out what that sound was. He should see if his parents were okay. He should be brave.

Instead he turned on his heel and ran for the front door.

He didn't make it.

From the dining room doorway, a figure lunged out, holding a small canister in one hand. There was a sharp hiss, and Jack felt a wet mist hit his face. Pepper spray!

He gasped and gagged, eyes stinging, his mouth and

throat on fire. Somehow he managed to get his backpack off his shoulder and swing it wildly at his attacker, though he could hardly see them through the tears. His legs were kicked from under him and he crashed to the floor hard. Terrified, he tried to scramble away, but he was seized and pushed facedown. In seconds, his wrists were tied behind his back, and he was helpless.

He stopped struggling and lay still. His face felt like it had been stung by a hundred bees at once, and his throat burned like he'd downed a jar of mustard.

His attacker rolled him over onto his back and stood over him. Through squinting eyes, Jack made out a tall, lean man in a black tracksuit and sneakers. He had a stern face and a sterner haircut, and a small mustache trimmed with laser precision.

"An attack can come at any moment, Jack," he said. "You must always be prepared. Always."

"Yes, Dad," Jack wheezed. "Can I have a sandwich now?"

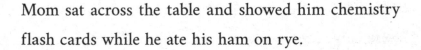

Mom sat across the table and showed him chemistry flash cards while he ate his ham on rye.

"Helium?" he guessed as she held up another baffling diagram of letters and lines.

"Sodium bicarbonate," said Mom. "Otherwise known as baking soda." She was square-jawed, short-haired, and blonde, and she wore a tracksuit the same as Dad's. They always wore the same thing. They didn't believe in fancy clothes.

She lifted up another card.

"Mffghmff," Jack said.

"Don't talk with your mouth full," Mom told him. "You'll choke. If the airway to your lungs is blocked, the oxygen supply to your brain will be cut off, and you'll die. Is that what you want?"

Jack shook his head, wide-eyed. He hadn't really considered the possibility of death by sandwich before. He swallowed very carefully and laid it aside, his appetite gone.

"Now, what's this?" she said, tapping the card. "Come on, this is an easy one."

Jack frowned, trying to make sense of the pattern of connected letters. He was sure he'd seen this one before. "Er . . ." he said. "Is it . . . cheesium?"

Mom gave him an *are you serious?* look.

"Cheesium's not a thing, is it?" Jack said, realizing his mistake.

"No," she said dryly. "It's not a thing."

"Froomium?"

"Now you're just making up words."

"I'm not! I'm not!" he said desperately, racking his brain for the answer. "Wait! I got this! I remember now!"

"Yes?" his mom asked, brightening.

"Meltium bidroxide!" he cried triumphantly.

Mom's face fell slowly. She put the flash card back on the table with a snap. Jack sagged.

"Zero out of ten," she said. "And even that was an improvement on last time."

"I still say you can't deduct points for fidgeting."

"This isn't a joke, Jack."

"Sorry," he mumbled, ashamed.

 She began to gather up the cards. "You know, you're eleven years old. Nearly twelve. Most boys your age can name at least a hundred chemical compounds."

"I'm not sure that's true—"

"And recite the complete works of Shakespeare."

"Actually, I don't think they ca—"

"*And* do calculus and complex algebra."

"I don't know anyone who can do tha—"

"What happened to you, Jack? Why aren't you trying?"

The disappointment in her voice gave him a little sad ache in his stomach.

"I *am* trying," he said. But no matter how hard he tried, he never even got close.

"Finish your sandwich," she told him, getting up from the table. "You'll need the energy."

Jack picked up his ham on rye, eyed it warily, then dared to try a tiny bite. She was right, of course. He needed to keep his strength up. After dinner he would have to run the assault course out back, and when he couldn't do it fast enough, he would have to do it over and over until Dad gave up. Then there would be target shooting, some survival training in the woods, and lastly a pop quiz on astronomy or physics or something. He would do badly at all of them. When they were over, he would collapse into bed, tired, bruised, and feeling like a failure. He would sleep, and wake, and it would be a whole new day, same as the day before.

In the brief time between lying down and falling asleep, he would sometimes imagine another life, with other parents who didn't act like drill instructors. A life where they did fun things together, like going out for burgers, or watching TV, or playing board games. A life where they didn't move every year to a different city. A life where he had a family and a place he belonged.

But he didn't have that. He had this. So he finished his sandwich and headed out to the yard, where Dad was already waiting by the assault course, checking his watch and tapping his foot.

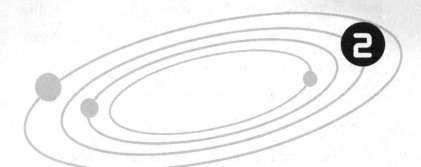

The class sweltered in the drowsy heat of the afternoon. Air-conditioning ducts groaned and rattled overhead as they fought a losing battle against the summer. Outside, a handful of unfortunates slogged their weary way around a baseball diamond in temperatures hot enough to melt the fillings in their teeth.

Jack scribbled at his desk, barely listening to the teacher, who was talking about a book the class had studied last semester. Everybody except Jack, of course. He'd been at a different school last semester, in a different state. Every time they moved, he found himself out of step with his fellow pupils, falling further and further behind. After a while, there didn't seem to be much point trying to keep up.

Instead he drew monsters, or aliens, or occasionally alien monsters. His pencil flew across the page, creating fantastical landscapes with a few flurrying lines, amazing worlds where magnificent cities lay under foreign stars.

In his imagination, he saw them as clearly as if he were standing there. He felt the winds of other planets on his face, smelled the scent of weird purple grasses and giant fungus forests. Whenever he tried to capture them with his pencil, it was only a pale copy of what was in his mind, but he drew them, anyway. And with every new picture, he got closer, he got *better*.

Drawing was something he was good at. Sometimes he thought it was the only thing, which made it even more important. When he was drawing, there were no tests, no exams, no one to grade him, or judge him, or tell him to try harder. No one to tell him he'd failed. When he drew, it felt right.

Mom and Dad didn't think art was much use to anyone. Not like science, or learning knots, or being able to recognize four dozen kinds of edible plants in the woods. So he drew at school instead, or on the bus home, or whenever he could. He needed to. He had to get the pictures out.

Since the teacher was paying him no attention, he began to flip through his sketchbook. As he had gotten older, he had begun to give names to the places and people he imagined. That was the watery, beautiful world of Gallia; there were the crafty Jumbahs, selling their wares in a shadowy bazaar; that was the Gigakraken, terror of the oceans.

He turned another page, and a shadow seemed to pass over him. He felt a chill despite the heat of the day. Staring back at him was a hunched figure, a tangle of flesh and machinery, with a fanged metal jaw and crazed yellow eyes. One arm was a huge steel claw, and there was a glowing pump made of pipes and tubing where a heart should have been.

He called them Mechanics. Sometimes he wondered why he drew them at all, since he always found them unsettling. But like all his pictures, they seemed to spring from his pencil of their own accord.

He closed the sketchbook and scanned the room. Long experience of being the new kid had made him a keen judge of character. By the end of the first day, he had already decided who would make friends and who would make fun. Usually he tried to buddy up with someone right away; it was good to be in a group, and it helped keep the bullies off him. But he had kept to himself this time around. He just couldn't face making a whole new bunch of friends again, only to wave good-bye the next time they moved. Besides, ever since he'd turned eleven, his dad had taken to ambushing him in public, and it was hard to make friends when your father kept carrying out mock assassinations on you.

But there was one of his classmates who he couldn't ignore. He found her on the other side of the room, listening intently to the teacher, scribbling down notes. Jodie Ellis.

He sighed quietly to himself. Just the sight of her provoked a strange yearning in his chest. Every day he admired her from afar, fascinated by her cheekbones, the curve of her chin, the effortless grungy cool she projected. She radiated an aura of *leave me alone*, which made Jack want to do the opposite.

I should introduce myself, he thought. *Go and say hi*. It was going to be a long way to summer break if he didn't make some friends.

Maybe he would. Maybe he'd do it today.

. . ✦ . .

By the time the bell rang at the end of class, Jack's stomach was in a tight knot. He darted up from his seat like he was on springs, and made it out the door before anyone else could get there.

The halls were flooding with students as he emerged. He hurried to the lockers and selected a spot next to Jodie's. It was the ideal place to accidentally-on-purpose meet her. "Oh, hey, I was just hanging out here," he'd say. "Wait, is this *your* locker?" Then he would charm her with some witty comment he had yet to think of. But he hoped something would come to him soon, because he was fast running out of time, and she was already walking down the corridor toward him.

At the sight of her approach, his mouth went dry. His brain flatlined. What would he say? What would he *do*?

Talk to her, he told himself. *Talk to her now!*

He drew in a breath. Something would surely come to mind. All he had to do was speak. All he had to was—

"Jack! Hi, Jack! I've been looking all over for you!"

Jack's face froze and his heart sank. He knew that voice. He pretended he couldn't hear it, desperately hoping its owner would just go away. Jodie was almost at her locker; it was now or never.

Say something!

"Jack! Hey, Jack!" He felt a tug on his arm. Slowly he turned his head, wearing a fixed grin of horrified disbelief.

"Thomas," he said, with a gaze that could have blistered paint.

Huge, watery eyes peered back at him through thick glasses that hovered uneasily on pasty, chubby cheeks. A thatch of black hair perched on his head, greasy and badly cut, as if he'd done it himself in a mirror. He was wearing a huge grin and an eager expression, like a dog pleased to see its master. A thin trickle of glistening snot leaked from one nostril.

There were cool kids. There were uncool kids. And then there was Thomas. Thomas had elevated being uncool to an art form. He was the Zen master of uncool. And he had decided that Jack was his new best friend.

"So what's going on?" Thomas asked in a high, breathy voice that sounded like he had a blocked tube somewhere. "I thought we could hang out at lunch, since you don't have any other friends yet."

Jack felt himself curl up and burn like a blowtorched slug. All thoughts of talking to Jodie—*ever again*—turned to ash. Her eyes skated over them both without interest as she opened her locker. He felt her dismissing him. If she had been at all curious about the new boy before, she wasn't now.

I'm Thomas's friend, Jack thought despairingly. *That's how I'll be known all through the school. Thomas's friend.*

He couldn't be near her anymore. It was too embarrassing to be in her presence a moment longer. Without a word, he walked away.

Thomas followed, of course, trotting alongside as Jack pushed his way through the groups of pupils that crowded the corridor. Thomas was immune to hints, didn't understand embarrassment, and was almost impossible to shake off. He was like the Terminator of social awkwardness.

They'd met on the first day, or rather, Thomas had ambushed him. Jack had been wandering the hallway, looking lost, when Thomas introduced himself and immediately started talking like they were old friends. Jack had humored him at first, thinking him weird but harmless. He didn't want to be rude, after all. Little had he known then what he was in for.

"Hey, so I was thinking, it's Saturday tomorrow," said Thomas. "You wanna go out riding bikes?"

His voice was way too loud. Jack cringed at the thought that Jodie could still hear him. Some older kids smirked as he passed, red-faced, shoulders hunched, Thomas twittering away at his shoulder. He picked up speed, walking as fast as he could go. Thomas struggled to keep up.

"If you don't have a bike, you can borrow one of mine; I've got one that's got three gears and it's got, like, speed stripes down the side, which the man in the store says makes it go faster, but I don't actually believe he—"

"Yeah, sorry, I can't do Saturday," Jack said tightly.

"Why not?" Thomas asked. He gave a loud snort as he hoovered a gobbet of snot back up his nose and wiped the rest away with the back of his wrist.

Jack, flustered and annoyed, couldn't think of anything to tell him but the truth. "It's my birthday, that's why!" he snapped, and immediately regretted it.

Thomas's face lit up and his eyes went wide, magnified to terrifying size by his glasses. "Your birthday? Great! So you're having a party?"

"No," said Jack, still trying to outpace him. "My parents don't do parties."

Thomas halted and looked aghast. "No party? On your *birthday*?"

Jack kept walking, almost at a run now. "That's right. Gotta go! Bye!"

He turned a corner and scooted away. The last thing

he saw of Thomas was his big chubby face looking sad, eyes swimming with pity.

Don't feel sorry for me! Jack thought angrily. *I'm supposed to feel sorry for* you*! You're the tragic one, not me!*

But then he thought of Jodie and wondered if that was true, after all.

He closed his eyes and took a deep breath. Yes, it really was going to be a long way to summer break.

Jack's twelfth birthday began when his dad leaped onto his bed, screaming like a plunging eagle, and delivered a flying elbow drop to his stomach. Jack was dragged out of bed by his legs, still fighting for breath, and dumped in the corridor, where his mom was waiting with a power hose.

"No, Mom . . . Just give me . . . a second . . ." he panted, holding out a hand to stop her.

He got no further. A blast of water slammed into him, sending him skidding up the corridor. He crashed into the wall at the far end and was pinned there, spluttering and thrashing. By the time Mom switched it off, he was battered, bruised, and half-drowned.

He raised his head, coughing, and wiped sodden hair from his eyes. Mom and Dad, dressed in identical black tracksuits, watched him with that familiar look of disappointment on their faces.

"An attack can come at any moment," said Dad. "Happy birthday, Son."

. . ✦ . .

Happy birthday didn't actually extend to getting presents, or a card, or a cake, or a party, or anything else you were supposed to get on your birthday. A birthday in Jack's house was just like any other day. He didn't even know when his parents' birthdays were. He wondered if they knew themselves.

They made him mop up the corridor and then they headed out for supplies, leaving him to fix his own breakfast. Dad had a plan to extend the assault course in the backyard, plus they needed bullets for target shooting, and more powdered food for the apocalypse shelter they were digging in the woods. Also, they had run out of milk.

Jack crunched dry cereal at the kitchen table and stared miserably out through the patio doors. His stomach ached where his dad had whacked him, and his hair was still damp from the hose. Outside, the sun was shining and there was no breeze to stir the trees behind the assault course. It was going to be another hot day. That would make the day's training all the more unbearable.

He hated that assault course. There were ropes to scramble through, walls to climb over, crawl tubes. There were heavy sacks of sand that Dad would set swinging, which he had to dodge through. Wooden poles set at different heights for him to jump over. A balance beam. A muddy trench with netting over the top.

Day after day his dad put him through his paces while Mom saw to his education. If he had been an athlete or a genius, he might have been able to keep up with their demands. They didn't seem to realize that he was neither.

Other parents weren't like this. Other parents did nice things for their kids, encouraged them, gave them treats now and then. Some kids liked their parents. Some even said they *loved* them.

Jack didn't know what that was like. His parents had always seemed like strangers who just happened to be looking after him. He was supposed to love them, because they were his parents, but he never seemed to get it quite right. Sometimes he wondered if there was something broken in him, something that stopped him feeling the way he was meant to feel. He tried to please them, he wanted to make them like him, but on some deeper level, some element was missing, and it pained him.

Maybe he was just a bad kid. He was always letting them down, after all. Perhaps they'd be nicer to him if he just tried harder.

The doorbell rang. He raised his head, briefly interested, but he didn't get up. He wasn't supposed to open the door when Mom and Dad were out. It was probably just a salesperson, anyway.

The bell rang again, but he was no longer paying attention. He was looking out at the woods behind their house. In his mind, the trees had turned into

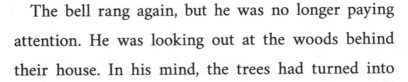

giant purple ferns, and beyond them he heard the swooshing waves of a great sea. The sea of Gallia.

Wouldn't it be great if it were real? If he could go there? To leave all this behind and travel to the worlds he drew in his sketchbook, to see the wonderful cities he imagined, with their gleaming spires and flying machines?

It was nice to dream. But soon Dad would be back, and the assault course was waiting.

A sharp knock on the patio door made him jump. His eyes bulged. Standing in the backyard, balancing a cake in one hand and wearing a huge smile, was Thomas. The sight of him made Jack choke on his cereal, and he coughed a spray of Rice Krispies across the table.

Thomas pulled open the patio door without waiting for an invite and thumped Jack hard on the back with his free hand.

"All right! I'm fine!" Jack cried when Thomas kept thumping him long after he'd finished coughing.

"Saved your life!" Thomas grinned. "Nobody answered the front door, so I came around the back.

Here, I brought cake!" He plonked it down on the table. "It's lemon soufflé. I got it from the Ezy-Mart. And now for the piéce de résistance!"

He produced a candle with a flourish and stabbed it into the top of the cake, which deflated with a lemony wheeze.

Thomas regarded the cake proudly. "There! Now, do you have something . . ." A strange look passed over his face. "Something to . . ." His nose wrinkled and twitched. "Something to light it wi— AaaAAAA-CHOO!"

Jack threw up his arm to cover his face as Thomas sneezed all over him, and the cake, and most of the kitchen table.

"Sorry," said Thomas, sniffing. "Allergies. All this pollen." He waved a hand toward the woods. "Do you have a cat?"

Jack, still aghast at being coated in someone else's mucus, could only shake his head.

"I'm allergic to cats, too. And dogs. Most animals, actually. And bees, er, well, they make me die." He pulled an inhaler from his pocket and sucked it sharply. "Plus I got asthma," he added with a wink, as if he was letting Jack in on a secret.

"You . . . you have to go," Jack managed at last.

"What? No, I just got here. It's time to get this party started!"

"Listen, my mom and dad, they don't let me have friends over, okay?"

"They don't let you have *friends*?"

"No, they let me have friends, they just . . . don't let me bring them back home."

"Why not?"

Because the ability to form short-term social relation-ships is advantageous in a survival situation, but deeper emotional connections are baggage. That was what Dad had told him, the one time he'd asked. Kind of a weird response, but then most of his responses were kind of weird. Jack sometimes wondered if the real reason they kept moving was to make sure he never got to pick up any "baggage" like that.

He caught himself. What a ridiculous thought. As if his parents would keep moving all over the United States just to stop him from making good friends! Dad's work meant that he got relocated a lot, to be near whichever office needed him; that was all there was to it.

"They just don't like it," said Jack, exasperated at having to explain something he couldn't even explain to himself. "Anyway, they'll be coming back soon, and if they find you here, they'll make me do that assault course, like, twenty times at least, and after that . . . Wait a minute, how did you even know where I lived?"

"Followed you home once," Thomas said absently, investigating the kitchen cabinets. "Oooh, you've got a smoothie maker!"

Jack didn't know how to put into words how creepy that was. "Okay, you know what? Thanks for the cake, it's super kind of you, but you really have to go—"

"You like it?" Thomas hurried excitedly back to the table. "I knew you were a lemon soufflé kind of guy!" he cried, waving his hands around as he spoke. "The lady in the shop said carrot cake was the safe bet, but I said, 'Oh, no! I know my friend Jack!' And then I—"

His flailing hands hit the cake and sent it sliding across the kitchen table to the far side. Both boys sucked in their breath as it teetered on the edge. It kept them in suspense for what seemed like an absurdly long time, then it tipped over and landed on the floor with a tired *whumph*.

"Oops," said Thomas.

Jack didn't mind that he'd killed the cake—he wasn't going to eat it, anyway, after Thomas had sneezed on it—but the thought of his mom coming back and finding a mess on the floor put him in a cold sweat. He'd be doing jumping jacks for a month.

"I have to clean that up," he said, hurrying to find a dustpan and brush.

"I'll just have a look around, then," Thomas twittered.

"No! You need to go!"

"Hey, this is a neat house!" Thomas called from down the corridor.

Jack dithered with the dustpan and brush in his hand, caught between the need to clean up and the desire to get rid of Thomas. In the end, the cake seemed like the simpler task.

"Don't touch anything!" he shouted as he scampered across the kitchen to scoop up the ruined cake.

"Is this your dad's office?"

"Stay out of there!"

He tidied up frantically, muttering under his breath. How could one kid manage to be so annoying? He glanced at the clock, and his heart lurched. It was later than he'd imagined. Mom and Dad would be back any minute.

He was just dumping the last of the crumbs into the garbage disposal when he heard a muffled crash from overhead. He dropped the dustpan and brush, and ran. What was Thomas doing upstairs? You couldn't take your eyes off that kid for a minute!

He found Thomas on the landing, standing guiltily next to a shattered painting that was lying on the floor. It was the only picture his parents had put up in the house, a bland watercolor they'd picked up at Walmart. It wasn't worth much, but it would still mean a whole heap of trouble for Jack. His muscles ached as he thought of how many times they'd make him run that assault course when they got home.

"Why were you touching that?!" Jack yelled in disbelief.

"I have an inquiring personality. Hey, what's this?"

"What's *what*?" Jack snapped, but Thomas was already opening the small panel set into the wall that the painting had previously covered.

"There's a button," said Thomas, and before Jack could say anything, he pushed it.

There was a creak from overhead. Farther down the corridor, a hatch in the ceiling popped open, and a ladder unfolded down to the floor.

"Cool!" Thomas said. "An automatic attic hatch!"

"We have an attic?" Jack said.

"Didn't you know?"

Jack shook his head.

Thomas's face lit up suddenly. "I bet that's where they're keeping your presents!"

"I'm not getting any presents. I never get any presents."

"Nah! It's your birthday! *Everyone* gets presents on their birthday!"

"Don't go up there!" Jack told Thomas as he started climbing the ladder.

"I'm just gonna take a quick look," said Thomas, disappearing through the hatch.

Jack gave a strangled howl of frustration and followed him. When he got to the top of the ladder, he found Thomas standing there, openmouthed.

"Whoa," said Thomas, his eyes filling his glasses. "Check it out."

Jack stared. The attic was huge and dim. A narrow sunbeam slipped through a skylight, setting floating dust particles afire. Occupying the shadows were several strange devices, glittering with tiny green lights that blinked and shifted. One looked like a console of some kind, but its design was sleek and menacing. Another was a large black ball standing on five legs, which displayed a row of strange symbols that changed as they marched across its surface. Still another looked like a cluster of spikes with ghostly light shimmering along its edges. Whatever they were made of didn't look like metal or plastic. It was as if they had been molded from liquid darkness.

Jack had never seen anything like them.

"You don't find these in Best Buy," said Thomas, awestruck.

"What *is* all this?" Jack asked in amazement as he climbed off the ladder. The devices all seemed to be on, though he couldn't see any plugs. Where were they getting their power from?

"Are your parents, like, government agents?" Thomas asked. "Because this is some next-level tech right here."

Jack's instinct was to say no. How could they be? They were just two fairly boring people in tracksuits who made him do stuff he didn't like. But hadn't he always wondered? Hadn't he always had that sneaking feeling that something was off, that there was something bigger to be found, some greater purpose behind the training and constant upheavals?

Occasionally, when he was younger, he'd made attempts to investigate, looking for some pattern in their strange behavior. He'd daydreamed that his parents were more than they seemed and that he had some great destiny that they would one day reveal. But he never found a thing, and after a while, he'd dismissed such thoughts as fantasies and stopped looking.

Now, staring at these machines, he wondered if he just hadn't been looking hard enough. His stomach fluttered with excitement, or fear, or both.

Thomas had squatted down in front of the cluster of spikes and was studying it closely.

"Don't touch anything," Jack warned him. "We don't know what it does."

"I'm not gonna touch it; I just want to look," said Thomas. "That looks like something you should press," he said, pointing.

"*Don't—*"

Thomas pressed. The device began to hum loudly, and the eerie light flickering around the spikes became brighter and turned a sinister bloodred.

"That doesn't look good," Thomas observed.

"Will. You. Stop. Touching. Things," Jack said through gritted teeth.

"I just want to get it back to how it was before. Maybe this button?"

Jack lunged at him to wrestle him away from the

machine, but he wasn't fast enough to stop Thomas from pressing it. Thomas tripped with a yelp as Jack grabbed him, and the pair of them tumbled to the floor.

The hum became a shrill whine, getting higher and higher, the sound of power building.

"Now look what you've done!" Jack cried. "It could be a bomb or something!" The fact that it wasn't out of the question that his parents had a bomb in the attic made him realize just how little he really knew of them.

"Let me press something else!" Thomas begged, pawing the air in his desperation to mess with it further.

"You've pressed enough buttons for one day!" Jack said, holding him back.

The colors of the spikes shimmered and shifted, bathing the attic in strange hues that made Jack feel slightly ill. His skin crawled with the energy that filled the air. The whine became a squeal, then a shriek, until Jack and Thomas had to clamp their hands over their ears. Small objects began to skitter about the attic, little screws and bits of metal that leaped up in the air and spun around as if caught in a twisting wind. Still the noise grew, until Jack didn't think he could bear it anymore, and then suddenly—

Silence. The tension went out of the air. The screws and bits of metal fell to the ground and rolled away.

Jack and Thomas raised their heads. The device was glowing a pure, bright green. A beam of light, the same color, projected directly upward from the cluster of spikes.

Thomas squirmed away from Jack and hurried over to the skylight, where he could see out. "It goes through the roof!" he said. "Right up into the sky!"

A moment later the device went dark. The light and the beam disappeared. Thomas's face fell.

"Oh," he said.

Jack picked himself up, staring at the device. "What, er . . . happened?"

"It made a beam of green light shoot up into the sky," said Thomas.

Jack was kind of put out by that. After all that noise, he'd expected more than a glorified spotlight.

"Let's do it again!" said Thomas, heading back toward the spikes.

Jack intercepted him. "Noooooo, no. We're not messing with anything else up here."

"What about *that* one?"

"Thomas," said Jack, his face serious. "Let's say my parents *are* government agents. What do you think they'll do to us when they find us up here?"

Thomas thought about that for a moment. "Shoot us?" he ventured at last.

"I would think they'd *start* by shooting us. God knows what they'd do after that."

Thomas swallowed uneasily. "Yeah, maybe we should get out of this attic."

"Right."

"I might go home, actually."

"That sounds like a good idea."

They closed up the attic and went out front so Thomas could get his bike. Jack scanned the street for his parents' car, but there was no sign of them yet.

"Sorry about the cake," said Thomas.

"No problem," said Jack. He was struck by an

unexpectedly touching thought, which took the edge off his annoyance a little. "Hey, you know, that was my first birthday cake ever."

Thomas grinned. "See you on Monday," he said, then wheeled his bike around and wobbled off down the road.

Only when Thomas was out of sight did Jack allow himself a sigh of relief. Just being near that kid stressed him out. He was a walking disaster zone. Jack was going to get it for that smashed picture. His birthday would be one long day on the assault course in the punishing heat, because of Thomas.

But as he went back into the house to hang the broken picture back on the wall, he couldn't stop thinking about what he'd seen in the attic.

Mom? Dad? Who are you?

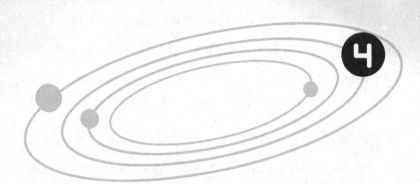

4

Jack thought he'd get in trouble when his parents found out about the broken picture, but they seemed more concerned with how it had happened. He told them he'd tripped against it.

"And did the picture fall off the wall?" Dad asked. He and Mom exchanged a glance that they thought he didn't see. "Is that how the glass broke?"

"No," said Jack innocently. "I just hit it with my elbow. Sorry."

They seemed uneasy for a moment. Then, as one, they broke into broad smiles.

"No harm done," said Mom. "As long as you're not hurt."

By the afternoon, the picture had been replaced with a different one, even blander than the first. They didn't even punish him. Jack was slightly frightened by that.

. . ✦ . .

In the week that followed, Jack looked for any opportunity to get back into the attic. He needed to find out more about those weird machines and what his parents were doing with them. But his parents never went out together, except for a supply run every few weeks. Even when he wasn't being trained or taught, there was always someone nearby.

Frustrating as it was, Jack told himself to bide his time and watch. Now that his suspicions were raised, he looked at his parents with new eyes.

"I mean, I just thought they were a bit weird, right?" he told Thomas at recess. "Like, I've just got weird parents. But this is more than weird."

Thomas sucked on a Slurpee, slobbering up the last few drops with a noise like a congested walrus. They were sitting on a wall in a remote corner of the school-yard where nobody ever went. Jack didn't much want to be seen with Thomas, but he had no one else to talk to about what had happened, and Thomas was the only one who would believe him, anyway. It was a depressing state of affairs, all in all.

"They've never been sick a day in their lives. Can you believe that? I can't remember one single day they were ill."

"What? That can't be right," Thomas told him. "Even government agents get ill. Maybe you're just forgetting." He took a suck on his inhaler.

"The other day, my mom was in the bathroom for ages. There's only one thing she can be doing in there, right? But I went in right after, and it didn't even smell!"

"That's just a parent thing. My mom doesn't poop, either."

"What, at all?"

Thomas shook his head.

"Well, it's still weird," Jack said. "And yesterday, my dad wanted me to do this new route through the assault course, so I pretended not to get it and I asked him to show me. He ran the course, and I said, 'Can you do it one more time, so I remember?' So he did it again. At the end of it, he wasn't even breathing fast. He wasn't even *sweating*, and it was, like, ninety-six degrees and the kind of humidity where you dry off by taking a bath."

"So he's a super-fit government agent," said Thomas. "We already know that. You're not focusing on the important stuff. We need to get back in that attic!"

Jack threw up his hands. "I've tried! They're always around!"

"Why don't you sneak up at night?"

"Too risky. Their bedroom is next to mine and they hear better than bats. The moment I open the door, one of them pops their head out."

Thomas frowned, tapping his heels against the wall. "You said you've only seen them wearing tracksuits, right? Nothing else?"

"That's right. Those stupid black tracksuits and sneakers. They must have a dozen pairs each. They think choosing different clothes every day is a waste of brainpower."

"So when they poke their heads out of their bedroom at night, they're wearing their tracksuits?"

Jack shrugged. He'd never thought about it before. "I guess," he said.

Thomas waited for Jack to catch on. He didn't.

"So, uh . . . do your parents *sleep* in their tracksuits or something?"

. . ⊹ . .

That night, before he went to bed, Jack drank three big glasses of water. He wasn't allowed a phone, and his alarm clock was too loud, so this was the best way he could think of to make sure he woke up in the night. It worked, if anything, a little *too* well. When he woke up at 2:05 a.m., he was on the verge of wetting himself.

He got out of bed and waddled gingerly through the dark to the door of his bedroom, afraid to take large steps in case he burst. He listened and heard silence beyond.

He turned the doorknob as quietly as he could and opened the door. Half a second later, the door to his parents' room opened, and Dad was standing there in the gap.

How did he get out of bed so fast? Jack wondered in amazement. Hard on the heels of that thought came another, which put a chill down his back. *Was he just standing behind the door the whole time?*

"Can't sleep?" Dad asked. "You should get some rest. You need to be sharp for training tomorrow."

"I need to pee!" Jack squeaked, jigging on the spot.

"Go on, then," said Dad.

Jack sprinted down the corridor and slammed the door of the bathroom behind him. There was a loud groan of relief from within. When he came back out, Dad was still standing there, watching.

"Good night," Dad said.

"Good night," said Jack, and he went back into his bedroom. A moment later, he heard the door to his parents' bedroom close.

He stood there in the dark, wide-awake now. There was no chance he was going back to sleep after this.

Two o'clock in the morning. His dad had still been wearing his tracksuit and sneakers. And despite the fact that he was supposed to have been lying on a pillow all night, there was not a hair out of place on his head.

There was no sign of Thomas at school the next day. *Probably out sick,* Jack thought. There was always something wrong with that kid.

Jack was half-relieved and half-disappointed. He was desperate to tell somebody about last night, but every day he spent with Thomas made it less likely he'd ever have any normal friends with non-runny noses and basic social skills. And though it was actually kind of nice to have someone to chew over the mystery with, he didn't want to spend the rest of the school year with only Thomas for company. He'd go insane within a month.

With no one to talk to, he kept his head down in class and drew in his sketchbook. This time, it wasn't the landscape of a different planet, or one of the many alien races he'd invented. Today he was inspired to draw something different. A huge flaming bird, flying through space, burning like a star. When it was done, it seemed somehow menacing. He imagined it searching the galaxy, looking for something, like a bird of prey seeking out a mouse. After a moment, it started to make him feel uneasy, so he closed his sketchbook.

Jodie Ellis was looking at him from across the classroom. He caught her eye, and she looked away.

.. + ..

When he got home, he stole a small wrench from his dad's tool kit and hid it in his sock. Mom tested him on calculus—he didn't do well—and then they had dinner. While they were eating, he excused himself to go to the bathroom.

"You've been going to the bathroom a lot lately," Dad observed.

He held up a glass of water and drained it. "It's important to stay hydrated, Dad!" he said.

"Very sensible, in this heat," Mom said approvingly.

Jack went upstairs, past the toilet, and into his parents' bedroom. Everything in there was as neat as a museum. There were no ornaments and no pictures, and the bed was perfectly made. Even a furniture showroom had more life in it.

44

He slid the wrench under the blanket. Then he hurried to the bathroom, flushed the toilet, washed his hands, and went downstairs again.

He was so tense when he returned to the table that he didn't want to eat any more. He forced himself, anyway, so as not to seem suspicious. He felt like he was wearing his guilt all over his face, but if his parents noticed anything, they didn't show it.

They finished their dinner, and then Dad took Jack out for some wilderness survival training. By the time they got home, it was dark and Jack was exhausted, so he went to bed. There he lay awake, listening, as his parents made their way upstairs to their bedroom. At any moment he expected the door to fly open, and Mom and Dad to be standing there, demanding to know how a wrench had gotten into their bed. It was impossible to miss it, after all. Even if they didn't see it at first, one of them would certainly feel it when they got in.

He waited and waited. Nothing happened. At some point, sleep overtook him, and he never even noticed.

. . ✦ . .

He jerked awake when his alarm went off for school, panicked briefly at the noise, and finally managed to swat the clock hard enough to shut it up. In the quiet that followed, he heard Mom clattering about down-stairs, making breakfast. Dad was hammering in the backyard, building new tortures on the assault course. Morning sounds. It was a normal day, just like any other.

Jack got up. He pushed open the door and listened again. Once he was sure that the coast was clear, he slipped into his parents' room. It was neat as always, the bed perfectly made, with hardly a wrinkle in it.

With a mounting sense of dread, he pulled back the covers.

The wrench was there, just where he'd left it. His parents had spent the whole night in this room, but they'd never noticed it.

They hadn't found the wrench, because they hadn't gone to bed.

5

"I'm scared of them," he told Thomas at recess. "I'm scared of my parents."

Thomas nodded thoughtfully, chewing a bar of peanut brittle. Jack had guessed right: He'd been out sick yesterday. He'd stepped barefoot on a slug while coming down the stairs in the morning, and the cold, squishy shock of it gave him an asthma attack. Thomas's life was full of little misfortunes like that.

"It's as if they're different people now," Jack continued. "When they smile at me it feels fake. All this . . .

normalness, it's just an act. Underneath, they're something else. I just don't know what."

"Government agents," Thomas said wisely.

"Will you drop it with the government agents?" Jack cried. "They don't go to bed! Even government agents have to sleep!"

"Depends which government," Thomas said with a cryptic waggle of his eyebrows.

Jack gave up on persuading him. "I don't want to go home," he said. "I'm not sure I can face them."

Thomas's face lit up. "Well, it's Friday, isn't it? Come and stay at my house for the weekend!"

Jack looked into Thomas's big, hopeful eyes, magnified to vast saucers by his glasses, and his heart sank.

We're not going to be buddies, he thought. *Sorry, but we're not. Just because you're the only person I can talk to about this doesn't make us BFFs.*

It made him feel bad, but there it was. To choose Thomas would be to choose *only* Thomas. His aura of profound dorkiness repelled other humans. He didn't seem to have any other friends, which meant that even other dorks wouldn't go near him. That was definitely a bad sign. If it wasn't for the secret they shared, Jack would be avoiding him like the plague.

"So? You wanna?" Thomas was jigging up and down with excitement. "My mom won't mind. In fact, she won't even notice." The excitement dimmed on his face, like the sun going behind a cloud. "She doesn't notice much that I do. Or anything, really. As long as the TV's on . . ." His voice trailed away and he stared off into the distance.

"My parents would never let me go," Jack said with mock regret in his voice. Even if they would have, he didn't want to accept. Going to Thomas's for a sleepover would make it impossible to extract himself when the time came.

Thomas focused again and clutched Jack's arm, an earnest look on his face. "We have to get you out of that house!" He wiped a glistening trail of goo from his upper lip, studied it for a moment, then rubbed it into his skin like it was moisturizer. "What if they do experiments on you?"

"I don't think they're going to do experiments on m—"

The bell rang before Jack could protest further, and Thomas sprang to his feet, scooping up his Hulk backpack. "I'll see you after school!" he yelled as he ran off toward his class. "We'll work it out! Sleepover!"

Jack sagged. Suddenly, facing his parents didn't seem so terrible, after all.

· · ✦ · ·

Going home was all he could think about for the rest of the day. What would he say when he saw Mom and Dad? Would they see through him? He *had* been acting weird at breakfast; he couldn't help it. Did they already suspect he knew about them? Would he come home to find a black van waiting to take him away? Or did they have something worse in store?

What if they do experiments on you?

What if they drank his blood? Or killed him and put him in a box? Or did something weird to him with those strange machines, like deleting his memory or controlling his mind?

It was hard to imagine them as enemies. As much as he'd struggled to connect with them, they'd always looked after him. Even his endless training was some sort of misplaced parental attempt to protect him, by teaching him survival skills that he'd never need. He'd never felt love for his mom and dad, but they'd always provided him with safety. He hadn't realized how much he valued that till it was gone.

What might they do if they found out he'd seen what was in the attic? Who were they, really?

When the bell rang at the end of the day, he was slow to get up from his desk. The other kids hurried off, but he dragged his feet and was the last one out.

"You took your time," said Jodie Ellis when he finally emerged.

He stared at her, dumbfounded. Jodie Ellis had been waiting outside his class. Waiting for *him*.

"Uh . . . hey!" he managed.

"Your name's Jack, right?"

"Right," he said, still somewhat dazed. "You weren't in class."

"Skipped it. English is boring."

"I thought you liked it? You're always taking notes."

She looked confused for a moment, then a spasm of irritation crossed her face. Jack worried that he'd said something wrong, but she shrugged off the question. "Whatever. You want to hang out?"

"Now?"

"Yeah, now. Come on, let's take a walk. I want to get to know you."

"You do?"

She rolled her eyes. "Do I have to spell it out? I like you. Or at least, I like what I've seen so far." She swatted him on the arm with the backs of her fingers. "Don't screw it up, okay?"

Jack broke out in a goofy grin. He couldn't help it. It was almost too good to be true. Jodie Ellis was the prettiest girl in the school as far as he was concerned, and definitely the coolest. Jodie Ellis wanted to hang with him? Jodie Ellis *liked* him? It was as if all those missed Christmases and birthdays had come at once.

"Hey, Jack!" Thomas called.

His grin trembled at the edges. *No, please, not again!*

Thomas hurried up to them, panting. He looked from Jack to Jodie and back again. "Ready to go?" he asked.

Jodie gave Jack a dry stare. "He's with you?"

Jack was fighting to stop himself from strangling Thomas right there. "I wouldn't say *with* me . . ."

"Sure I am!" Thomas said. "Come on, Jack! We gotta make plans!" He turned to Jodie. "Jack's parents are government agents who don't ever sleep!" he explained eagerly. "We've got to get him away from there till he can find out about the secret machines in their attic!"

Jack was still smiling to disguise the screaming inside. Jodie turned slowly to Jack and gave him a long look. "Government agents, huh?"

"It's not like it sounds," Jack said feebly.

"Yes, it is," Thomas said, bewildered.

"No," said Jack through gritted teeth. "It isn't."

"Yes," said Thomas, as if talking to an idiot. "It is."

"NO IT ISN'T!" Jack yelled, unable to contain himself anymore.

"YES IT IS!" Thomas yelled back, waving his hands around like an electrocuted monkey.

Jodie looked bored. "Hey, Thomas. You need to take a hike, okay? Jack and I are going for a walk, and you're not invited."

Thomas smirked at that. "Don't be silly. He's my best friend! We're gonna—"

"Fat boy!" she snapped, her voice sharp as a whip. "Go!"

Thomas's smirk faded. He looked at Jack with the wounded air of a recently kicked puppy. "Jack?" he said, his chin beginning to tremble.

Jack shrugged awkwardly. "I'll see you around, I guess," he said. Then Jodie pulled on his arm and guided him away, leaving Thomas stunned and staring in the corridor.

"Why do you hang out with that loser, anyway?" Jodie asked as they left, loud enough for Thomas to hear.

Jack didn't reply. He hated to admit it, but he felt terrible for blowing off Thomas like that. The kid was a pain in the butt, but he didn't deserve to be treated meanly. It was just that it had come down to a choice between the coolest girl in the school and the uncoolest boy.

No contest, really.

Around the back of the school was a little path that ran off through the woods. It followed a small stream for a while and eventually came out among the condos near the swimming pool on Clark Street. The kids who lived over that way used it as a shortcut, but Jack had never explored it until now.

Insects rattled and cheeped in the sweltering heat. Even under the shade of the branches it was too hot to think. Jack and Jodie walked side by side, the stream splashing past to their left, neither of them speaking. Jack racked his brain trying to think of something to break the awkward silence, but his brain was not cooperating.

"You've been watching me in class, haven't you?" Jodie said suddenly, casting him a sly sideways look.

That sounded a bit stalkery to Jack. "I would say *observing with interest.*"

"I've been watching you, too." She handed him her cell phone. "Wanna see?"

"Uh . . . sure," said Jack uncertainly. The cell phone was a brand he'd never seen before, sleek and black and expensive looking.

A video popped up on the screen, showing grainy footage from a camera. He felt a chill as he recognized himself, hanging out uneasily by Jodie's locker. Thomas came running up, and while Jack was trying to get rid of him, Jodie opened her locker, ignoring them both.

It was from that day when he'd tried to say hello to her, and Thomas had ruined it. The whole scene, caught by a security camera in the hallway.

"That's . . ." He fought to find something positive to say but couldn't. "That's just really creepy. How did you get it?"

"They keep the computer mainframe in the control room of the lab. All the camera records are there."

"It's a *locked* control room, though."

"Whatever. The point is, I've been watching you watching me. That's how I knew you liked me."

She gave him a mischievous smile. Jack tried to smile back but couldn't quite manage it. This girl he'd admired from afar was not so entrancing close up. She was beautiful all right, and cool, but it was the cruel kind of cool, and that made her less beautiful. Plus there was this whole spying thing. It was impressive that she'd managed it, but it was weird all the same.

By now they had come to a small clearing by the stream, where several paths met, some heading deeper into the woods. There was an old mossy log lying on its side, and birds were twittering in the trees.

"We're here," she said.

"Where's here?"

She turned to him and laid a finger on his lips. "Do you want to kiss me?" she asked.

Jack suddenly forgot all that stuff about her being cruel or weird. His face glowed and his heart began to thump hard. He nodded mutely. She smiled at his nervousness, stood on her tiptoes, and leaned toward him. He closed his eyes and—

"Jack!"

His dad cannoned into him with a scream like a kamikaze owl, tearing him out of Jodie's grip and sending them both tumbling to the dirt. They rolled over and over until they finally came to a stop some distance away, with Jack lying on his front, pinned beneath Dad's weight. Mom was also there now, aiming a toy ray gun at Jodie that looked like a reject from a *Star Trek* cosplay.

"*No!*" Jack screamed, pounding his fist on the ground. "Now is *not* the time for a mock assassination! God, you guys are *so embarrassing!*"

Neither of them was listening. Mom had her eyes fixed on Jodie, staring down the sights of her ray gun. "Back away, Hunter," she said. "He's not for you."

"You're threatening her with a toy gun!" Jack yelled. "Could you *be* any more ridiculous?"

Then he saw what was happening to Jodie, and he shut his mouth.

An evil, hungry leer had spread across her face, an expression that did not seem to belong to the girl he had adored. She was making a quiet hissing sound, and a thin, bad-smelling steam was rising from her body. As Jack watched in horror, her features began to melt and run together like hot wax.

"Two Guardians?" she gurgled. "That's all you have to defend you? *Please.*"

She thrust out her hand, and it became a long, bladed tentacle that lashed out like a whip toward

Mom. Mom rolled aside and came up firing her ray gun. Two sizzling bolts of energy flew through the air toward Jodie—or whatever it was that had pretended to be Jodie—but a moment before they hit, two gaping holes opened in her body, and the bolts passed harmlessly through.

The creature that had been Jodie drew the tentacle back into its body like it was slurping up a noodle. By now it had melted into a huge oily blob, shimmering with strange colors, blorping and oozing toward Mom.

"I was going to kiss *that*?" Jack squeaked as Dad pulled him to his feet.

"Get up!" Dad barked, in a voice more serious and commanding than Jack had ever heard before. "You need to run."

"Run *where*?"

"Anywhere!"

A blazing bolt of red energy shrieked out of the undergrowth and hit Mom square in the back.

"Mom!" Jack yelled.

She staggered in place. A smoking hole had been blasted right through her. Tubes dangled in the gap, squirting white goop; smashed canisters and crystals leaked little puffs of glowing gas. They were the same eerie colors as he'd seen coming off the spiky device in the attic.

Jack turned to his dad in shock. "You're androids?"

"I prefer the term 'artificial person' myself," said Dad prissily.

Jack thought for a moment. "You know, this explains a *lot*."

Mom tipped over and crashed to the ground.

"A hit, by Jove! A very palpable hit!" cried a buzzing voice from the trees. Into the clearing stepped a lanky robot with thin metal limbs and a tall tube-shaped head. He was wearing a monocle over one mechanical eye, a top hat, a tweed jacket, and riding breeches, and he carried a huge shiny blunderbuss in both hands. A drooping mustache, lopsided and off-center, was stuck in the middle of his face.

"TOF-1 and the Changeling," Dad muttered. "That means Scorch won't be far behind." He drew a ray gun identical to Mom's. "It's you they want. Go. I'll hold them off as long as I can."

"They want *me*? What have *I* done?"

They heard a crashing in the trees behind them, the sound of something heavy thundering closer.

"Go!" Dad shouted.

Jack didn't wait around any longer. He sprinted across the clearing, ducking as an energy bolt seared over his head, and plunged into the trees.

Behind him, he heard his father open fire.

6

Branches whipped and scratched at Jack as he staggered through the undergrowth, running headlong into the woods. From the clearing he heard the screams of TOF-1's blunderbuss and Dad firing back. Somehow he knew Dad didn't have a chance. He'd heard it in his voice. *I'll hold them off as long as I can.*

He had been saying goodbye.

Mom. Dad.

No wonder he'd never been able to love them the way he was supposed to. He'd sensed on some deeper level that something wasn't right. They weren't his parents. They weren't even human. What had the Changeling called them? *Guardians.*

His head whirled with confusion and terror. It was too much to take in. All he could do was run, and keep running.

Because there was someone following him.

He heard them behind him, smashing through the branches as if they were matchsticks. Heavy, thumping footsteps on the turf. Closer and closer.

Dad had mentioned a third name. *Scorch.* Why was his pursuer called Scorch?

A jet of flames spewed through the forest, setting leaves afire and turning trees to smoldering black pillars that splintered and tumbled to the ground.

Oh. That's why, then.

He tripped, tumbled to the ground, and scrambled back up again. Through the smoke, he caught a glimpse of a hulking shape striding closer. Panic welled within him and he fled, running through the woods at reckless speed, desperate to get away.

The ground disappeared from beneath his feet. Suddenly he was falling, bouncing, rolling down a steep slope he hadn't seen coming. Brambles scratched at his face and arms, and he knocked his head on a tree root. At last he skidded to a stop at the foot of the slope in a tangled heap, gasping and dazed.

A stream of roaring flames cut through the forest above him. He covered his head and squeaked like a frightened possum as burning branches dropped to the ground all around him. When he raised his head, he found he had not been hit, but it seemed that everything around him was on fire.

A flaming tree creaked nearby. Jack clambered to his feet and got out from underneath a moment before it crashed down in a blazing pile of leaves and timber.

Coughing, he ran onward, deeper into the woods. Scorch came thumping down the slope after him.

The woods became thicker, branches knotting together. He ran this way and that, sweating in the heat, until he came up against a wall of twigs and brambles that blocked his way. He looked over his shoulder—could he turn back?—but Scorch was closing in on him, a bulky shadow in the smoky murk.

No time. Instinct took over. He scrabbled under, crawling on his knees and elbows through the mud.

Just like on the assault course. Just the way Dad taught me.

And suddenly he knew. All that training, all the lessons they'd put him through and the knowledge they'd tried to impart. It was all for today, for the day when the Hunters came. All so he could run fast, be smart, escape, and survive.

He wished he'd listened harder now.

Jack emerged from under the brambles. More branches crossed his path in a tangled maze. He climbed into them, squeezing through the gaps the way he'd learned to do on the rope nets. It was hard work, but he was used to hard work. Behind him he heard Scorch tearing up the forest, close on his heels, but Jack had found his focus now.

Make a plan. Survive.

Then he was through the branches, and now there was a rocky cliff rising before him, thirty feet high. He ran at it without thinking twice, found a handhold, and began to climb. Up, up, up he went, like he'd done a hundred times on the climbing wall. His muscles strained, but he was strong enough. By the time Scorch broke through the branches behind him, he was over the top and running again.

Frantically he tried to come up with a tactic. He was lost in the woods, and he didn't know if he could outrun Scorch. His pursuer just battered through any obstacles, and that cliff wouldn't stop him for long. And Dad had taught him how to deal with angry bears or hungry coyotes, not fire-spewing monsters. At least, he'd tried to; the lessons didn't often stick. What *were* you supposed to do if a bear was chasing you?

Then it hit him. *Climb a tree.* If he couldn't outrun Scorch, he'd hide from him.

He found a likely looking candidate and scrambled up into it. Somehow his hands and feet found all the right places, and soon he was high up among the branches. He nestled into the crook of a bough and went still. Immediately it occurred to him that maybe a tree wasn't the smartest place to hide from someone who was burning everything in sight, but by then it was too late to do anything but stay put and hope.

From the direction of the cliff, he heard a creak of

metal and a lumbering step. Scorch was out there, looking for him.

He walked slowly now. Listening, perhaps. He didn't know where Jack had gone and was waiting for him to give himself away. Jack clung tighter to the branch and held his breath.

Please don't find me, please don't find me—

Then, through the leaves, Jack saw him.

He wore an enormous suit of black power armor, covering him from toe to neck, which whirred and buzzed as he moved. Huge three-fingered gloves gripped a massive, dirty flamethrower, which was attached by a pipe to a fuel tank on his back.

But it was his face that was the strangest; or rather, the lack of it. His head, if he had one, was covered by a transparent dome rising from the neck of his armored suit. Within the dome was only a thick cloud of gas and smoke, swirling red and black, flashing now and then with hidden lightning. Visible through the gas were two glowing chips of light—Scorch's eyes—but nothing else could be seen of the thing inside the armor.

He stomped closer, until he was standing directly

below where Jack hid. Sweat beaded on Jack's brow. He could smell sulfur and the reek of fuel. If Scorch looked up, it would all be over.

Don't. Look. Up.

Somewhere off in the woods, a branch cracked loudly, as if someone had stepped on it, and he heard a muffled grunt. Scorch straightened, alert, and hurried off in that direction.

Jack dared to take a breath again. He listened as Scorch plowed off through the trees. When he sounded far enough away, Jack began to climb down. Instinct told him to stay hidden, but there was always a chance the others would come searching after they'd dealt with Dad. Better to get as far from here as possible.

He checked to make sure the coast was clear, then dropped to the ground and dusted himself off.

"Hey," said a voice behind him. He whirled around and was hit by an energy bolt straight in the chest.

The next thing he knew he was slapped hard on the face. He jerked awake and found himself lying on the ground, looking up at the branches overhead. Bright sunlight forced its way through the leaves and the drifting smoke from the nearby fires. His whole body ached, his cheek hurt, and his head was pounding.

A girl wearing purple overalls, her hair dyed half a dozen colors, had her hand raised to deliver another slap. She lowered it with a look of slight disappointment as she saw his eyes were open.

"Well, he's awake, just about. You did set it to *stun*, right?"

A man, in his late thirties by the looks of him, came to stand next to her. He had black hair and a black beard, both clipped short, framing a wry brown face. "Might have put the power a bit high," he said. His voice was deep and smooth.

The girl knelt down and examined Jack closely. Rows of glowing symbols hurried across her eyeballs in a line, followed by a blur of diagrams. It went by so fast that Jack wasn't sure he'd seen it at all.

"He's not permanently injured. Won't be able to move for a while, though."

Jack didn't much want to move, even if he could have. He just wanted to lie there and wait for the pain to go away.

"You all right in there?" the girl said, waving a hand in front of his face. "One blink for yes, two for no."

Jack thought about that for a moment, then blinked.

"Okay, good. I'm Mazzy, and this is Boston."

"Boston Sark," said Boston. "Bounty hunter. Smuggler. Adventurer. You might have heard of me."

Jack blinked twice.

"Well, now you have," said Boston. "I just captured you. Tell your friends."

"Are we leaving or what?" rumbled another voice. "Won't take Scorch long to work out it was me who lured him away."

Another man stepped into view, or at least he was *like* a man. He had a flat wide face, a shaggy beard, big ears, and a forehead like a cliff, and his skin was the color of clay bricks. It was as if a bodybuilder had been squashed in a mechanical press until he was almost square: four feet tall and four wide.

"Just waiting for you, Dunk," said Mazzy. "Let's go."

"Who wants to haul the prisoner back to the Epsilon, then?" Dunk said. "Must be someone else's turn to be the mule. Any volunteers?" He looked from Mazzy to Boston. Mazzy and Boston looked back at him. "I see. Old Dunk here gets to carry him, is that it?"

"You're twice as strong as both of us put together," Mazzy said.

"That's not the point," Dunk grumbled. "This is exploitation, that's what this is."

"Maybe we can talk about this somewhere we're not in danger of getting killed at any moment?" Boston suggested, scanning the trees.

"Oh, it's never the right time, is it?"

"Just pick him up!" Boston snapped.

Jack felt himself lifted as if he weighed no more than a blanket. Unable to move any part of his body, he flopped limply over Dunk's shoulders like a slain deer. The strange little man was hard as oak and burning hot— Jack could feel the heat radiating through his clothes. He smelled faintly of boiled cabbage and old socks.

They set off through the woods, Jack jogging against Dunk's back. Boston had a blaster in his hand, keeping an eye out for anyone following. Mazzy hurried alongside, her eyes scrolling with numbers and symbols.

"We're losing the rift," she said. "It's becoming unstable."

"We'll get there," said Boston. "I'm not getting stuck on this dirt ball planet for weeks, I'll tell you that!"

"I hate Earth," Dunk complained. "Just being here makes me feel dirty."

"You *are* dirty," Mazzy told him. "There's stuff in your crevices that's been there since before I was born."

Dunk scratched behind one big ear and pulled out a flaky blob of something sticky. He held it up next to Mazzy, as if to compare it. "How old are you again?" he asked.

They came into a rocky clearing on a slope, a small patch where no trees grew.

"Epsilon!" said Boston. "Where are you?"

"Here I am," said a soft female voice that seemed to come from nowhere. The air shimmered in front of them, and out of nothingness, an aircraft swam into view.

Jack's jaw would have dropped if it hadn't already been hanging open from the paralysis.

The Epsilon was a thing of beauty, a long, sleek needle with swept-forward wings and engine casings along its flanks that glowed with a soft green light. It stood on five skids, towering over them, and there was an entry ramp in its belly that was lying open.

"Welcome back, Boston," it said.

They hurried over to it and up the ramp. As they went, Jack caught sight of something in the trees behind them. It was hard to see properly since his head bounced with every footstep Dunk took, but it looked like . . . it *looked* like the front wheel of a bike, poking out from behind a tree.

Why was there a bike out here in the woods?

There was no more time to wonder about it, because now they were inside and hurrying down a dim corridor. The walls were covered with mysterious panels, little blinking lights and transparent cylinders that swirled with strange energy. Boston made his way straight to the cockpit at the end, and the others followed.

The cockpit was large enough to accommodate several seats, a complicated dashboard, and a dozen screens of various sizes, some of which were showing views of the outside. One of the seats was occupied by a tall, thin young woman wearing a black cloak, with the hood pulled up over her head. She turned to them as they entered. Her face was beautiful and delicately boned, her skin light gray, her eyes bright yellow and slitted like a cat's.

"The mighty hunters return," she said scornfully. "You managed to capture a twelve-year-old boy, then?"

"Hey!" said Boston. "This twelve-year-old boy is one of the most dangerous spies in the Nexus!"

Jack blinked frantically, but nobody noticed.

"Shackle him to a chair," Boston told Dunk. "If he tries to escape, you have my permission to punch his face into the next plane of reality."

"Roger, boss," said Dunk.

"Epsilon, make ready to leave."

"Retracting ramp now," came the infuriatingly calm voice of the aircraft.

"You don't need to announce every step of the process," said Boston.

"Ramp closed. Lock engaged. Entry secure."

"Epsilon, what did I say?"

"Engaging engines."

"Just hurry up!"

By now Jack had been dumped in a swivel chair, sitting the wrong way in it so his chest leaned against the backrest. He could do nothing to resist as Dunk handcuffed him to it.

"Gghhh" was all he could say, since his lips didn't work.

"Couldn't have put it better myself," Dunk told him. He gave Jack a slap on the back, nearly dislocating a rib, and stomped out of the cockpit. "I'll be in engineering," he told the rest of them grumpily. "Like always."

Mazzy ignored him; she was scanning the screens. "No sign of them yet," she said.

"Soon as we get up in the air, they'll be after us," said Boston. "Strap in, everyone. Epsilon, take us up."

"Ascending."

"Hunter craft decloaking to starboard!" Mazzy cried.

"Already?" Boston muttered, working at the dashboard. "That was fast."

"Must've realized they lost their target and headed back to their craft."

"Boost it, Epsilon!"

"Engaging boost—"

"Oh, forget it. Manual control."

"Are you sure?" The computer sounded hurt.

"Yes, I'm sure," said Boston through gritted teeth.

"Pilot has manual control."

The engines roared, and everyone was flung back against their seats. Jack slithered and slumped against his chair as the cockpit shuddered and shook. Out of the corner of his eye, he saw the gray-skinned woman watching him with a tiny smile on her lips.

Who are you people? he thought in terror.

How nice of you to ask. My name's Ilara, a voice replied in his head.

Jack goggled at her.

"Mazzy, get on the console!" Boston snapped. "I need specs on their craft. Tell me if we can take 'em!"

Mazzy reached over to the console next to her, pulled out a thin cable from her wrist, and plugged it into an input. Glowing lines of data raced across the surface of her eyes.

"Give me an assessment of our chances," he barked at her.

"It's a Viper-class combat model with elyrium

engines and LADAR-guided micromissiles." She pulled the cable out, and it retracted into her wrist. "We're doomed," she said chirpily.

"Not if I can help it," said Boston, and Jack felt himself flattened as the Epsilon went into a steep climb.

Jack was getting some of the feeling back in his arms and legs now, and he could move a little again, enough to stabilize himself against the back of the chair. He swiveled around to see the cockpit, after one last suspicious glance at Ilara. Surely he hadn't really heard her voice in his mind?

Through the main window he could see blue sky and fluffy clouds. Smaller screens showed the view from the sides and below, the woods dropping away beneath them, his school, the town shrinking as they climbed. Lifting off from the woods was another aircraft, dirty black, blocky, and brutal. The Hunters, coming after them. Coming after *him*.

What did I do? Why are they chasing me?

Ilara frowned slightly, her catlike gaze still fixed on him.

"The rift is breaking down," Mazzy said urgently,

scanning through data feeds. "We're gonna lose it!"

"It just has to hold on a few more minutes," Boston told her.

An alarm sounded in the cockpit. **"The Viper has a weapon lock on us,"** the Epsilon informed them calmly.

"That might be a few minutes we don't have," Mazzy muttered.

Boston cursed and flung the Epsilon to port as energy beams sizzled through the air, close enough that the aircraft rattled and its screens lit up with alerts. Jack held on to his seat and tried to ignore the fact that Ilara was staring at him unnervingly.

"Missiles in the air!" Mazzy cried.

"Epsilon! Countermeasures!" Boston yelled.

"Releasing chaff," the Epsilon said, with the same unhurried tone as someone might use to announce a train delay, or call a cleaner to aisle three.

A cloud of sparkling metal flakes scattered into the air behind them. Jack watched on the screens as a dozen tiny missiles flew into them and exploded, making the Epsilon shudder again.

"The message said dead or alive, right?" Boston asked Mazzy.

"Uh-huh," she said. "I think they're definitely taking door number one on this one."

"Well, that's just great."

Dead or alive? Why would someone want me dead or alive? What's going on?

Oh, come now, Gradius, said Ilara's voice in his head. *Don't be coy. No need to pretend.*

My name's Jack! he thought back at her.

How tiresome. I'm a Host, as you well know. I can pull the truth out of your head if I have to.

But I'm not whoever you think I am! Jack tried to say it aloud, but all he could manage through his floppy lips was: "MmmMMmmUUURGGH!"

"The storm's ahead!" Mazzy called. Through the cockpit window, black clouds had filled the view. "Two minutes. We're losing that rift!"

"We lose that rift, we'll be stuck on this dirt ball planet till it opens again," Boston said, brow furrowed in concentration as he flew. "And I don't much rate our chances of survival then."

"Don't much rate them *now*," said Mazzy gloomily.

The clouds swallowed them. The cockpit dimmed and the Epsilon began to shake as it was battered by winds. Lightning flashed all around.

"Incoming!" Mazzy called. Boston flung the aircraft into another string of evasive maneuvers as the clouds lit up around them with streams of burning plasma. The Epsilon bucked and more alarms rang as the air filled with the smell of melting metal.

"We have sustained critical damage to the left thruster," said the Epsilon pleasantly.

A radio crackled. "Boston! This is Dunk! We've sustained—"

"—critical damage to the left thruster," Boston and Mazzy said in chorus.

"Don't know why I bother telling you anything," Dunk grouched, and the radio went dead.

"Boston, are you sure you've got this?" said Mazzy. "We can't take any more hits like that."

"I can outfly them!" Boston insisted.

"Why don't we put the Epsilon into Com—"

"Don't say it!" Boston warned her.

Mazzy thought for a moment. "But if we put her into C-O-M-B-A-T M-O-D-E," she said, spelling out the letters, "we might have a better chance of escape."

"Did somebody say *COMBAT MODE*?" the Epsilon shrieked.

"Fancy that," said Ilara blandly. "Our hyperintelligent onboard computer, capable of navigating us through nine-dimensional space, knows how to spell."

"Oops," said Mazzy.

"Ya-*HOO!*" the Epsilon screamed, and slammed hard to port, spiraling crazily. Jack was thrown off his seat, hanging on only by his manacles.

"Whaff haffening?" he groaned as the Epsilon spun into the heart of the storm.

"The Epsilon only ha-ha-has two modes of op-op-operation," Mazzy said, swaying wildly in her chair. "Ri-ri-ridiculously chill or hysterically psycho!"

"I think you mean *COMBAT MOOOOOODE!*" the Epsilon howled, slamming to starboard hard enough to rattle Jack's teeth. Plasma bolts scored the clouds around them.

"I could have flown her!" Boston protested, pinned in his seat, his cheeks rippling with the g-forces.

"Rift up ahead!" Mazzy cried.

Jack raised his head and saw the clouds part before them. There, hidden in the center of the storm, was a shimmering patch of light, pulsing with strange colors that made his eyes water. The clouds swirled around it like water down a drain, firing lightning into it.

"It's closing up!" said Mazzy. And indeed it was getting smaller by the second.

"Lock in destination coordinates!" Boston called. "We're going for it!"

"Done!"

They were slammed against their seats again as a new volley of plasma fire raked the sky. Jack watched on the screens as the Viper emerged from the storm, hammering through the air in pursuit. A dozen glowing lights detached from it and came streaming through the clouds toward them.

"More missiles!" Mazzy cried. "Where's the chaff?"

"**No more chaff!**" the Epsilon yelled happily. "**Hold on, everybody!**"

The Epsilon's engines bellowed. Jack hung on to his seat for dear life, his legs skidding around on the floor, as they raced toward the swirling lights.

"Impact in five seconds!" Mazzy yelled. "Four!"

The missiles streaked closer.

"Three!"

The light had filled the cockpit now, shining through the window, blinding him.

"Two! One!"

"Say goodbye to Earth, kid!" Boston yelled.

"Place was a dump, anyway," Mazzy muttered.

The air stretched like putty, and Jack screamed.

Bursts of steam hissed like angry snakes, and the air stank of engine grease and oil smoke. The corridor rang with clanks and thumps, the bang of hammers and the wheeze of pistons. Striding through it all, her boots clicking on metal grilles underfoot, came General Kara, her face stern as always.

What was left of it, anyway.

She was part woman and part machine, but how much of each only she knew for sure. Beneath her drab military uniform, pumps pushed fluid through pipes where a heart should have been. One hand was robotic, and half her face had been replaced, her left eye a narrow white slit. The human side of her face was as emotionless as the other, lightly lined with fifty years of not smiling. The eye there was dull and cold, her hair buzz-cut and gray.

She swept through the facility, surrounded by the restless industry of the Mechanics. They never stopped creating, constantly building new weapons and new recruits. But to create, they had to destroy, break things up to make them anew. The whole of the Nexus was fuel to them, raw material to be tossed into their furnaces.

She admired that about them. Their ruthless desire, their lack of weakness, of compassion. It was why she had joined them, why she let them change her. Most people lived in terror of being caught by the Mechanics and transformed into one of their cyborgs. Not Kara. She had volunteered.

A door squealed open and let her into the comms room, where several drones hunched over their consoles. They were mindless robot workers assembled higgledy-piggledy, all leaking joints and jerking gears. The Mechanics were expert scavengers, using and reusing whatever they could, and many of their creations were bolted together from junk.

A screen crackled to life as she entered. Scorch loomed there in the dim cockpit of the Viper, glowing eyes gazing out of the cloudy dome that sat atop the neck of his armor.

"You failed," General Kara said flatly.

Scorch's eyes burned more fiercely. He made an angry hissing noise, like a strong wind through the treetops of a forest. Words appeared on the screen, subtitles provided by the translation software.

THERE WERE COMPLICATIONS.

"Complications," said Kara flatly.

SOMEBODY GOT TO HIM FIRST.

"Somebody?"

A smaller inset screen appeared in the corner of Kara's display. Boston Sark stared out at her, a data feed displaying his information alongside.

WE IDENTIFIED THE AIRCRAFT.

Kara studied the data feed for a moment. "A small-time smuggler. Or at least that's what he seems. Is he working for Gradius Clench?"

PERHAPS HE WAS IN THE RIGHT PLACE AT THE RIGHT TIME. PERHAPS HE INTERCEPTED THE SAME TRANSMISSION WE DID.

"You mean he was already on Earth? What would he be doing there?"

SMUGGLING.

The inset picture switched to show Mazzy, her multi-colored hair growing wild around her face.

"She's from Rakkan," said Kara in faint surprise. "She must have escaped when the Mechanics invaded."

WHEN YOU LED THEM TO YOUR HOME PLANET TO ENSLAVE YOUR OWN PEOPLE, Scorch corrected her. Even through the subtitles, Kara heard the disapproval. It didn't bother her. Scorch was from Oma III, a gas giant planet where there was no solid ground. The Omians were intelligent clouds, like miniature storms, only able to live outside their home planet by traveling in armored suits. Kara wasn't about to be lectured by a whiff of gas.

"She had top-of-the-line wetware," Kara observed. "Computers integrated in her brain and eyes, allowing her to hack into electronic systems remotely. Must have had rich parents. Who else are we dealing with?"

The screen changed again to show Dunk, squat and frowning. His shoulders were so wide and his legs so short that he was practically a cube.

Kara studied the face. A Thuvian, from a high-gravity world where everything grew low to the ground. Thuvians were tough as stone and only a little smarter, but their talent with machines was second to none. This one must have fallen on hard times if he was working on a smuggler's ship instead of in one of the great Thuvian aircraft factories.

Last to be shown was Ilara, a Host from Cerinus Minor. That was a surprise. Hosts were arrogant sorts who thought themselves superior to everybody else. Mostly they kept their own company, but occasionally they became bored of being pampered and ventured out into the world searching for the kinds of interesting things that only happened to the poor and ignorant. She must have been *very* bored to stoop so low.

"Can you find them?" she asked Scorch.

WE HAVE THEIR ENGINE SIGNATURE. NEXT TIME THEY USE A RIFT, WE WILL KNOW.

"I'll put a bounty out on them. That ought to flush them out. They might even decide to give him up, once they realize who it is they have."

DO YOU THINK IT REALLY IS GRADIUS CLENCH?

A smile touched the edge of Kara's lips. "Does it matter? We're going to kill him, anyway, aren't we?"

With a wave of her hand, she blanked the screen and swept out of the room.

. . ✦ . .

The faint sharp light of a distant sun, colored purple by a toxic haze of smoke, shone through the windows as General Kara made her way to the Gristle Pits. As she walked, she turned things over in her head. Had Clench slipped up and revealed himself, or was this just a false alarm? That boy had been a thorn in her and the Mechanics' sides for a long time now. He needed to be put down before he caused some real damage.

As long as he didn't find out about the Firehawk, she thought. But surely he couldn't have. They were safe here, even from him.

A door clanked open as she approached, letting her out onto a balcony overlooking a large metal pit. Down below, a small figure dressed in black was being circled by a pair of beasts three times his size. They were Gristlers, nightmarish monsters fashioned by the Mechanics from metal and flesh, all oily claws and greasy jaws, seeping black smoke as they moved.

The beasts lunged together, surging in to rip their prey apart. Their target moved like lightning, somersaulting out of the way, and their jaws snapped shut on thin air. A blaster appeared in one hand, a blade in the other. Eerie colors swirled off it like mist.

The Gristlers turned and lunged again, but once more he was not where they thought he was. He leaped into them, firing plasma bolts, his blade swinging down to plunge into his opponents. The beasts fell on him hungrily, and he was lost in a snarling, shrieking tangle of limbs and claws. But his blade flashed left and right, cutting through the Gristlers' armor as if it were paper. Pale fluids squirted and machinery sparked as the creatures were cut to bits by the small warrior darting among them. Though they clawed at him desperately, they could not so much as scratch him. At last they slumped to the ground in twitching heaps, leaving their killer standing alone.

"Are you done exercising, Vardis?" Kara called.

He looked up at her. His face was a mirror, an oval of polished black metal, behind which no features could be seen.

"Good. I have news of Gradius Clench."

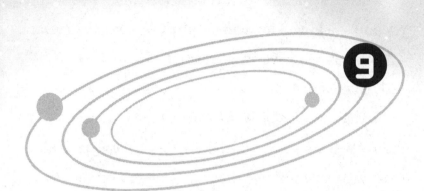

9

Jack howled as he was assaulted on all sides by scrubbing brushes, scrapers, shavers, and other things he couldn't identify, all whizzing around him on thin metal arms. Trapped inside the decontamination tube, naked as the day he was born, he had no way to escape them. There was a thick glass window at face height. Through it, he could see his kidnappers watching him.

"Quit probing me!" he squealed helplessly as he was poked and prodded in all kinds of unmentionable places.

"Oh, shut up," said Mazzy. "We all had to go through it. Even Dunk, and he almost broke the machine."

"There's filth, and then there's *my* filth," said Dunk proudly, picking a boulder of wax from one hairy ear.

"Why do we have to be decontaminated, anyway?" Jack complained.

"Because we've been to Earth," said Mazzy. "The most disgusting place in the universe. Eww, my skin's crawling just thinking about it. Unless I've got ticks." She looked at Boston, alarmed. "Can you see any ticks?"

"You mean in the entire universe there's nowhere more disgusting than Earth? There isn't, like, a planet of slime people or something?"

"The slime people are actually very nice," said Mazzy, sounding slightly offended. "And their slime is good for the skin."

"But what's so bad about it?" Jack said, moving his head to avoid a toothbrush that was trying to jam itself between his lips. "I mean, it's got nice parts!"

"It's because the whole planet is swarming with tiny invisible things whose only purpose is your horrible and painful death," said Boston patiently.

"Germs? What, don't you have— MmMMFF*ff*?" He was prevented from saying anything further when the robot arms clamped his head to keep it still and rammed the toothbrush into his mouth.

"No, we don't," said Mazzy. "Not like you do. Earth has the most vicious and nasty diseases in the Nexus. You have flesh-eating viruses, some that make your limbs go black and drop off, some that make you lose control of your body. Even just standing still you can catch the flu and die. And, I mean, the Black Death? Killed half the people in Europe? Who *does* that?"

"And that ain't even mentioning the animals," Dunk added. "We got great big monsters in the Nexus, but *you* have *spiders*. Tiny poisonous things that kill you with one bite. Poisonous frogs, poisonous jellyfish. Poisonous insects."

"Yeah, and Australia? Forget about it," Mazzy added. "Literally every living thing on that continent is trying to kill you at all times."

"The whole planet has been quarantined ever since it was discovered," Boston told Jack. "No one's allowed to come here."

The toothbrush was violently jerked from Jack's mouth. "So why were *you* here?" he managed to say, before he was blasted with hot steam from all sides.

"Because there are some things you can only get on Earth," said Boston, "and people will pay a lot for them."

Jack's reply was muffled by the top that was pulled down over his head by a half-dozen robot arms. He whooped in surprise as a pair of briefs were pulled up his legs and pants were yanked on afterward. In a matter of seconds he was dressed again, in new and unfamiliar clothes, and then the door hissed open and he was ejected out of the chamber. Dunk grabbed him and slammed his butt down on a chair.

They stood over him, glaring down. All except Ilara, who was standing off to one side, a wry half smile on her face. Jack looked around for a way to escape, but there was nowhere to go. They were in a chilly stor-age room in the hold of the Epsilon. The only feature other than the chair he sat on was the decontamina-tion chamber, sitting amid a mass of pipes and cables against one wall. The door to the room was sturdy and metal and locked.

"I don't know what you want. I'm just a kid," he said helplessly.

"Oh, sure," Mazzy scoffed. "A kid guarded by androids, with some of the nastiest Hunters in the Nexus after him. You must be very ordinary."

"They were my . . . my parents," Jack said, feeling terribly sad all of a sudden. Even one of Dad's ambushes would be better than this.

Boston, Dunk, and Mazzy exchanged glances. Then they burst out laughing.

"Nice try, Gradius Clench," said Boston. He mimed a crying face, rubbing his cheeks with his knuckles. "Boo-hoo, my parents!"

"My name is Jack," said Jack, his voice becoming hard. "Not . . . Grodius Clutch or whatever."

Boston rolled his eyes. "Mazzy? Show him?"

Mazzy slipped on a pair of goggles that looked like camera lenses. From her eyes, she projected a picture into the empty air, hovering in front of her. Jack stared as he saw himself there, beneath large red letters that spelled out WANTED FOR SABOTAGE, THEFT, AND TREASON.

Dunk whistled. "Treason. That's a big one."

"That's not me!" Jack cried. "I'm an American citizen! The most treasonous thing I ever did was switch channels during the Super Bowl!"

"It sure looks like you, though," said Boston.

"It's not me! *I'm* me!"

Boston held up his hand. "We get it, Gradius. You're in deep cover. You've been pretending to be a schoolboy for so long, you've started to believe your own story. Maybe you're lying low to escape your enemies. Maybe you mean to infiltrate some evil organization. Very cool. But can we drop it now?"

"*I AM NOT GRANTIUS CLUNGE!*" Jack screamed.

"GRADIUS CLENCH!" Boston yelled back. "AND YES YOU ARE!"

"No, he's not," said Ilara airily.

Jack pointed at her, as if to say: *See?*

"I looked into his mind while we were escaping. He's not Gradius Clench."

Boston seemed lost. "But . . ." He indicated the image hovering in the air, and then Jack.

"I know he looks like him. *Exactly* like him. But it's not him," said Ilara. "Memories don't lie. He's lived his whole life on Earth. He actually thought those androids were his parents. Also, he has a foul habit of leaving his toenail clippings on the floor."

"Hey!" Jack cried.

"Why didn't you say?" Boston asked Ilara.

Ilara smirked. "I thought it would be amusing to watch you flail around for a while. It turns out it's quite boring."

Mazzy, who had taken off her goggles, gave Ilara a nasty glare. "You know, your superiority complex can get kind of grating."

"Wait, I can prove it!" said Boston. He hurried out of the room and came back holding Jack's sketchbook, which had been in his backpack when he was captured.

"That's mine!" said Jack, rather pointlessly. He tried to get up to grab it, but Dunk shoved him back down again.

Boston flipped through the pages, showing them pictures. "Look! This is Gallia. Arcturus Prime. And *this* one is a Mechanic!" He brandished the sketchbook triumphantly at Ilara. "If he's never left Earth, how come he's been drawing things from all over the Nexus? Things he's never seen?"

"What's *that*?" asked Ilara, peering closer.

The page had fallen open at the last sketch Jack had done, of the enormous fiery bird flying through space. "How am I supposed to know?" Boston said.

Jack was amazed. "Are you saying . . . these pictures in my head . . . they're *real*?"

"Of course they're real," Mazzy said.

"Nevertheless," said Ilara, "he's not Gradius Clench."

"Who *is* this guy Globius Crutch?"

"GRADIUS CLENCH!" they all yelled at him together.

"All right," said Jack, slightly hurt. "No need to shout."

"Gradius Clench is a spy," said Mazzy. "They say he's the best in the business. He might only be a kid like us, but these past few years he's put a lot of noses out of joint. Powerful people. Nobody's sure who he works for, or if he works for anyone at all. Nobody's really sure what he's up to. But a lot of people want to get their hands on him."

"Do I look like a spy?" Jack asked.

"No," said Mazzy. "Which is exactly how I would expect a spy to look."

"You sent a distress signal!" Boston accused him. "Why did you do that?"

Jack was about to protest that he didn't send any kind of signal, but then he remembered the devices in the attic that Thomas had fiddled with. He remembered the beam of green light, shooting into the sky. "That was a distress signal?"

"Well, it was an alert of some kind, but we couldn't decode it," said Mazzy. "Hard-core encryption. We were still deciding whether to investigate when a bunch of Hunters turned up through the rift gate. I hacked their comms, and they were talking about claiming a bounty on Gradius Clench. So we thought—"

"We thought we'd get you first," said Boston, sulking a little now. "And after all that effort, turns out you're not even him." He brightened suddenly. "Hey, we could still pass him off as Gradius, sell him for the bounty, anyway?"

He looked around at his crew for support. Nobody gave him any.

"If he's not Gradius Clench, then he's innocent of whatever they want him for," said Mazzy. "Can't sell out an innocent person. Who knows what they'd do to him."

Boston looked like he was trying to think of some argument that might convince them that it would be okay. He didn't manage it.

"Great," he said, sagging. "So now we have the world's most useless hostage."

"We could put him back?" Mazzy suggested.

"I ain't going back to Earth," Dunk muttered. "You in a hurry to get decontaminated again?"

Mazzy eyed the decontamination chamber nervously.

"Doesn't matter," said Boston. "The rift to Earth is closed now. No telling when it'll open. Might be that the Hunters got trapped on Earth, or maybe they got into the rift gate in time. Either way, we can't go back. And I'm not sure our hostage here has much to go back *to*, anyway."

That struck Jack hard. Boston was right. Everything

was gone. If he went home, he'd be an orphan, and with no relatives or even any real friends, his prospects were bleak indeed. As much as his parents had been strange and disconnected, he missed them now. They had provided a life for him, at least. They had . . . *guarded* him.

His whole world had been ripped out from underneath him, and everything afterward had happened so fast that he'd hardly had time to make sense of it. He wondered whether he should be freaking out more about being chased by killer aliens, or being kidnapped from Earth through a hole in the sky.

But, try as he might, he couldn't dig up the panic he expected to feel. He wasn't particularly eager to go back to Earth. What was happening to him now felt more natural and right than his life back at home had been. He thought about the pictures in his sketchbook and wondered if, on some level, he'd always been ready for this.

But how did that make any sense? How did he *know*?

Boston sighed. "Toss him in with the other one. We'll figure out what to do with them later."

Dunk hauled Jack to his feet and began marching him out the door. "Wait! Wait!" Jack cried, but Dunk's

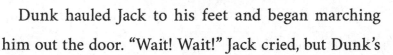

strength was incredible; it was like trying to resist a mountain. "What do you mean, *the other one?*"

"Caught him sniffing around the Epsilon," Boston said as he was dragged away. "Didn't have time for Ilara to blank his mind, so he had to come, too. Hey, you might have something in common. You're both from Earth. Won't find many more like you around!"

"What's his name? What's his *name?*" Jack cried, but Dunk had already pulled him out of earshot and was towing him down a corridor, muttering something about union rates and indentured labor. He palmed a door lock, and the door slid aside with a hiss, revealing a small cell beyond.

"In you go," said Dunk, lobbing him inside. The door closed behind Jack before he could get back on his feet.

"*Jack?*" said an eager, quivering voice in the gloom. "Jack, is that you?"

Jack turned slowly. He knew that voice. Suddenly he remembered the bike he'd seen in the forest.

Of all the people to be stranded with, not *him!*

"Jack!" cried Thomas, his pudgy face lighting up like the sunrise.

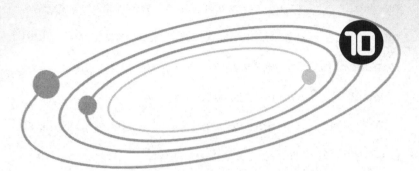

10

"Home, sweet home," said Boston sarcastically as he stepped off the loading ramp of the Epsilon and into the bustling airdock.

Jack and Thomas followed him, with the rest of the crew keeping a close eye on them. When they got to the foot of the ramp, they stood there and gawked.

It was like they'd stepped into a science fiction movie. Several dozen aircraft of all makes and sizes surrounded them, and none of them was anything like they'd ever seen on Earth. There were some that looked like crouched beetles, some that were thin like needles, and some that were so blocky and enormous that Jack wondered how they could fly. One looked as if it had been grown from seeds rather than built by hand. Walking between them were flight crews, passengers, dock officials. Only some of them looked human. The rest were very obviously not.

"Aliens!" Thomas breathed.

"This is Gallia, and you're from Earth," said Ilara at his shoulder. "*You're* the aliens now."

The airdock stood on a circular platform projecting out of an endless green sea. A huge yellow sun was rising over the horizon, peering through bands of clouds, setting them alight. A flock of strange seabirds winged overhead, calling in shrill voices. The airdock was attached by a bridge to a gleaming city of silver and steel that rose out of the ocean, towering above them, its spires scratching the sky.

This is Gallia, Jack thought in amazement.

He'd had a little time to think on the journey here, though not much, and Thomas's babbling hadn't made it easier to organize his feelings. Of all the people he could have ended up with, it had to be *him*, didn't it?

But as much as Thomas got on his nerves, he had to admit there was some comfort in a familiar face. Any port in a storm.

He'd expected Thomas—sickly, sniffling, pudgy Thomas—to be panicked and blubbering at the idea of being kidnapped. Thomas had surprised him with his resilience; in fact, he seemed more excited than scared about the whole thing. Judging by his behavior to date, he had a hard time grappling with consequences, and the idea that they might be in real danger had probably not occurred to him yet.

As for Jack, he felt it best to bide his time for now, until he could get a better idea of what was going on. It wasn't like he had much choice in the matter, anyway.

Keep your eyes and ears open, said Dad in his head. *Be ready to act when the time comes.*

Another spike of grief pierced him. He bit his lip. It bothered him that he cared. He *shouldn't* care. They were androids! Imposters! Whoever they were, they had lied to him all this time. Now that he'd digested that fact, it made him angry.

And there was something else he'd thought of, something that made him angry and dizzy and lost all at once.

If the people he thought were his parents were really androids, what had happened to his *real* parents?

"Sure you don't just want to leave the Earthers behind?" Dunk said. He was pulling a wheeled metal container the size of a dumpster behind him.

"I don't like leaving them on the Epsilon by themselves. No telling what they'll get up to. Anyway, you'll behave, won't you, boys?" Boston held up his hand, revealing a metal bracelet with a button on it.

Jack and Thomas nodded sullenly. Both of them had thin metal collars around their necks, capable of delivering painful shocks to the nervous system. Boston had already demonstrated how painful they could get, even though he hadn't really needed to. Jack suspected he was still miffed about kidnapping the wrong person.

"Remember, you've got nowhere else to go," he told them. "Come on. I've got some business to see to. After that, we'll work out what to do with you."

"Here comes the inspector," Mazzy murmured.

A uniformed man with no chin and a haircut you could set your watch to came striding across the dock. He stopped before them and eyed the container that Dunk was hauling.

"What do you have in there, then?" he asked.

Ilara stepped forward, her cat eyes intense, half a smile on her lips. "You don't want to look in there, Inspector," she told him calmly.

"Of course not!" said the inspector. "Why would I want to look in there? Off you go, now." He waved them past toward the bridge.

Thomas stared at Ilara in awe. "Did you just do a Jedi mind trick on him?" he gasped.

Ilara rolled her eyes and sighed.

They crossed over the narrow bridge toward the city, shining in the beautiful sunrise. Jack looked out across the sea, and his chest swelled with the air of this alien world. He was filled with wonder. *It's just how I imagined it*, he thought. *But how is that possible?*

"Pretty planet, isn't it?" said Boston, following his eyes. "It's not pretty where we're going."

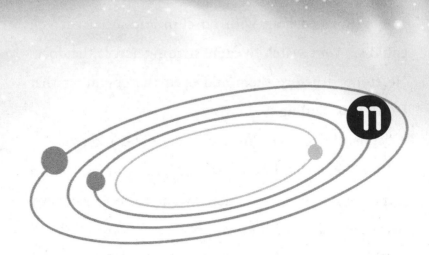

11

Gallia only shone on the surface. Up there, Boston told them, the rich lived in wonderful, elegant floating cities and wanted for nothing. For everyone else, there was the Underneath.

They took an elevator at the end of the bridge, down into the depths of the sea. Through the windows they could see out into the water that surrounded them. At first they watched reflective whales and colorful tentacled things propelling themselves through the sunlit water, but the sea became dark as they went deeper. Then there was only blackness, where luminous, nasty-looking things lurked, and they caught glimpses of huge creatures with too many teeth.

Thomas gabbled all the way down. He was desperate to tell the story of how he had come to be here, even though Jack had already heard it and the rest hadn't asked.

"I thought there was something funny about that Jodie girl. I mean, she must have done something to you, right, Jack? Like, some kind of mind control. Otherwise you wouldn't have let her talk to me like that."

Jack made a vague noise that could have meant anything. He was only half listening, anyway. The idea that he might have real parents somewhere had been growing in his mind, and he was beginning to get an idea of how he might start looking for them.

Keep your eyes and ears open, said the voice in his head again. *Be ready to act when the time comes.*

Shut UP, Jack thought resentfully. *You're not my dad.*

"Anyway, so I followed Jack and saw which direction he was going," Thomas told the others, "but I didn't have enough evidence to act on my suspicions, so I went back to the school, because I hadn't gotten my stuff out of my locker for the weekend yet. That was when I heard the commotion, and I found . . . Guess what I found?"

He waited for someone to ask him. Finally Mazzy stirred and took the bait. "What did you find?"

"Jodie Ellis! Someone found her unconscious in the girls' bathroom. They pulled her out, but they couldn't wake her up. It was like she'd been drugged or something."

"She was lucky. The Changeling doesn't usually leave its victims alive," said Boston.

"Probably didn't like the idea of getting Earth blood everywhere," Mazzy offered. "That stuff's swarming with infections."

"I knew I had to save Jack!" said Thomas, waving his hands around to get everyone's attention back on him. "I didn't know what was going on, but I figured it was something to do with government agents or something, so I jumped on my bike and headed off after him. I got into the forest and I heard laser guns firing or whatever, and I thought I'd better get off the path and into the trees so I could sneak up on them." He paused to take a blast on his inhaler. "Then I got a little lost and couldn't find my way back to the path."

"Yeah, excellent attempt at a rescue," said Jack dryly. "Thanks for that."

Thomas beamed. "You're welcome," he said, completely missing the sarcasm. "Anyway, I wandered for a while and ended up in a clearing, just in time to see you three appear from thin air!" He motioned at Boston, Mazzy, and Dunk. "I guess the Epsilon was invisible and you stepped off it."

"Right," said Mazzy. "And then you made this weird noise of surprise like a strangled guinea pig, and Boston jumped out of his skin and shot you with his blaster."

"I thought he might be the Changeling!" Boston protested weakly.

"Lucky it was on stun, that's all I can say."

"Yes . . . lucky," said Jack. "So why did you bring him on board?"

Boston shrugged. "Well, he'd already seen us, and we couldn't have witnesses. We weren't supposed to be on Earth at all. We were going to get Ilara to wipe the memory of us away, and then we could let him go, but things got hot after that and we never got the chance."

"Erasing memories is a delicate operation," Ilara said. "It takes time."

"So I got to go into space!" Thomas cried.

Boston motioned at the black depths around them. "Does this look like space?" he asked.

"A bit," Thomas said, shrugging. "It's dark, anyway."

"Nobody goes into space," said Mazzy. "It's a waste of time. Space is too big to get anywhere worthwhile before you die of old age. Even if you went at the speed of light, it'd take forever. And it's impossible to travel at the speed of light."

"Er, that's why they have *warp speed*?" said Thomas, snickering. "Don't you know anything?"

Mazzy pinched the bridge of her nose to fend off an impending stress headache. "This is not *Star Trek*," she said.

"Hyperspace, then!"

"Or *Star Wars*."

"So how *did* we end up on Gallia?" Jack asked.

"Through a rift gate," said Boston.

"Through a who's that now?" Thomas said.

"Rift gate," said Mazzy. "See, eleventy crillion years ago or whenever, some ancient race we call the Elders figured out that traveling through space was a dud move. So they sent twelve of these rift gates to various planets out across the galaxy. Maybe it took them a million years to get where they were going, maybe longer, but when they got there, they set themselves up automatically, and—*bam!*—A to B in an instant."

Thomas clapped his hands together in triumph. "Wormholes!"

Mazzy gave him a flat look. "Nobody calls them wormholes. That's such an Earther thing to say."

"Hey!" said Jack, who was getting a bit annoyed at the way everyone was picking on his home planet.

"Anyway, these twelve planets are called the Nexus. The rift gates are all connected, so if you know the coordinates of one, you can get to it from any other. That's how we got to Gallia from Earth. If the Hunters got through the rift before it closed, then they must have ended up somewhere else. What's important is that we lost them."

Jack was brimming with questions, but before he could ask them, a cheery, idiotic little ditty played in the silence.

Mazzy looked embarrassed. "Gotta change that ringtone," she said, then tapped a communicator behind her ear. "Go ahead, Epsilon. You're on speaker."

". . . RGENT NEWS . . . OUNT . . . EADS . . ." said the ship's computer calmly.

"Say again, Epsilon. You're breaking up."

"We're too far underwater," Boston murmured.

"URGENT N . . . GOING TO . . . YOU . . ."

The voice crackled into silence. Mazzy shook her head. "Lost the signal," she said.

"Don't much like the sound of that 'urgent' part," Dunk said.

"Well, let's do what we need to quickly and get back," said Boston as the elevator reached the bottom and the doors opened into the Underneath.

It was a far cry from the lighted world above. Down here it was dim, and broken lamps flickered. Metal tunnels leaked and creaked with the ominous weight of the water above them. There was trash piled in the corners, and shady characters coughed and muttered in the mouths of dark alleys.

"My old stomping ground," said Boston bitterly. "Say hello to the real Gallia. Bet you didn't draw *this* in your sketchbook."

They made their way through shady passages, an ugly world of rivets and steel where hungry-looking people lurked. They passed shabby markets and saw floodlit underwater fields where thousands of people in heavy diving suits labored among rows of colored seaweed.

"Here's where the work gets done that lets those above live in luxury," said Boston. "There are spices and plants that grow at the bottom of the Gallian ocean that you can't get anywhere else in the Nexus. Those workers don't last more than a few years before the weight of their suits and all that water mean they can't work anymore. But that doesn't matter to the folks above."

"Is that why you became a smuggler?" Jack asked.

Boston grunted. "Anything rather than end up here."

"What are you smuggling, anyway?" Jack asked. "I mean, you all seem to think Earth is such a hole. What's Earth got that everybody else wants?"

Boston gave him a suspicious look, as if deciding whether to trust him or not. "Reality shows," he said at last.

Jack wasn't sure he'd heard right. "Er . . . what?"

"Reality shows. *The Voice, Love Island,* all that kind of stuff. Nobody does them like Earthers. It's the only thing you're good at, apart from the amazing immune systems you've got from fighting off all those deadly germs."

"Reality . . . shows . . ." Jack repeated slowly.

Boston shrugged. "The Nexus goes nuts for them. What can I say? They're like a drug."

"And probably do as much damage to your brain," Mazzy added cheerily.

"Anyway," said Boston, "it's illegal to go to Earth, so either you have to wait a million years or so for the signal to reach you across space, or you have to get dodgy copies from someone like me."

Jack eyed the dumpster-sized container Dunk was pulling. "That thing is full of recordings of reality shows?"

"Whole seasons of *MasterChef India* in there," Boston commented proudly.

"Aye, and don't I feel it in my back," Dunk complained. "Here I am again, hauling a load like a mule. Just 'cause I'm a Thuvian, everyone assumes I'm the strongest. That's racist, that is. Ain't there some law about how much a feller's allowed to pull?"

. . ⊹ . .

Their destination, as it turned out, was a nightclub called Scoochy's. It lay at the end of a shabby alley off a deserted tunnel, where only one in three of the overhead lights was working. The name was written in swirly neon handwriting that hovered in the air above the forbidding metal door that guarded the entrance. It was quiet and looked closed.

Thomas glanced around nervously. "Doesn't this place seem a little . . . er . . . dangerous?" he suggested. He took out his inhaler and sucked on it.

"Danger is my middle name," said Boston.

"It actually is," said Mazzy, projecting a copy of his Gallian citizen's ID into the air in front of him. "He changed it."

"What was it before?" Jack asked.

"Marion."

Thomas snorted and choked on his inhaler.

"My parents wanted a girl," Boston said irritably.

Jack barely managed to suppress a smile. He wasn't supposed to like these people—they'd kidnapped him and Thomas, after all, and put them in torture collars, which was mildly unfriendly, to say the least—but against his better judgment, he was warming to them. Underneath all that bickering and griping, Jack sensed an easy, unquestioning companionship. They knew one another's faults and didn't care. They felt like a family, or at least what Jack imagined a family to be like. Jack couldn't help but be attracted to that.

Dunk lumbered up to the door and pounded on it with one huge fist. The ringing impacts faded into silence.

"Nobody home?" said Thomas hopefully, his eyes still watering.

The door screeched and began to move. Behind it was an enormous hairy alien who looked like a cross between a gorilla and a turtle, wearing a sharp suit and carrying a blaster in one meaty paw.

"I think your boss is expecting us?" Boston told him.

The gorilla-turtle grunted and waved them inside. Dunk dragged the container full of reality shows in behind him.

The interior of the nightclub was covered in battered fabrics. Curtains hid alcoves full of sofas, and there were strange ornaments on the tables. They were led through to the main dance floor, which was surrounded by a high balcony and lit by chandeliers of cloudy and scratched crystal. There in the center was the alien Jack presumed they were supposed to meet. Standing with him were half a dozen goons of various races from across the Nexus, some human and some definitely not, because they had tentacles coming out of their faces or something.

"Boston Sark! And you've brought your whole crew!" he said. "How pleased I am to see you."

He looked like a newt, with a long body draped in robes and smooth, glistening skin. A long blue tongue flickered out between his fangs and licked one of his bulging eyes. Wisps of black hair were slicked across his head in a greasy comb-over. There was something oily and deeply unpleasant about his manner, like a used car salesman or a Realtor.

"Hello, Gax," said Boston. "I brought the goods."

"Excellent!" said Gax. "I have buyers lining up for the episodes of *The Real Reality Show.*"

"Is that the one where it's a reality show where you watch people watching reality shows?" Thomas asked.

Gax seemed to notice Thomas for the first time, and then looked at Jack, studying him as if he were a particularly tasty fly. "Are these two *Earthers* you have with you?" he asked Boston. "How fascinating. You do like to pick up strays. And what's your name, boy?"

"I'm Jack," Jack said, then added defiantly, "Jack from Earth."

He may not have liked his home planet much while he was there, but it was part of him, just like his android parents were. He'd been moved from state to state so often that he'd never had a place he could have claimed to come from. But he came from Earth. He would claim that one.

"Jack from Earth." Gax wheezed with laughter. "I'm sure you are."

Boston didn't seem to like the sound of that. "Well, we're kind of in a hurry, Gax, so if you want to check out the merchandise, please do. But either way, give me my money."

Gax gave him an evil smile. "Your money? You must not have got the memo, Boston." There was the sound of a dozen blasters powering up above them. Jack looked up and saw goons gathered on the balcony that surrounded the dance floor, aiming at them.

Boston didn't flinch. "Really, Gax? Haven't I always come up with the goods? You're going to rip me off now?"

"Rip you off? No, you're too good a supplier for that." He motioned at one of his men, who produced a palm-sized projector. "Show him," he said.

An electronic notice projected itself into the air above the man's hand. On it were pictures of Boston,

Mazzy, Dunk, and Ilara. WANTED, said the message. DEAD OR ALIVE.

"There's a bounty on all your heads," said Gax. "A *big* bounty. The kind of bounty that makes losing your business worthwhile."

"Huh," said Dunk. "That'd be the urgent thing Epsilon was trying to tell us."

Mazzy gave Boston a dry look. "Did we just walk into a trap, Boston?"

"Yup," said Boston. "It's a trap. Hit the lights."

A sparkling line of code danced across the surface of Mazzy's eyes, and everything went black.

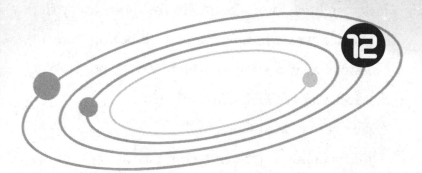

Jack had suffered enough ambushes from his dad to know what to do when the lights went out. He hit the floor and rolled as everyone began shouting in confusion and a few fizzing bolts of plasma scorched through the dark from the balcony.

"Stop shooting, you fools!" Gax screamed. "You might hit me!"

Boston Sark had no problem with that, however. The darkness lit up with muzzle flare as he fired his blaster randomly in Gax's direction. Two of Gax's goons went down, but Gax slid away like water, his long body winding into the blackness. Dunk piled forward into the rest of them, bulldozing them flat with his immense weight.

Jack caught sight of Thomas in the momentary flare of light. He was whimpering and gibbering, dancing on his toes as if uncertain which way to go. Jack got to his feet and grabbed Thomas's arm.

"Door is that way! Come on!"

Thomas clung to Jack in terror, pawing at him desperately as Jack pulled him clear of the fight.

"Now!" Gax shouted to the goons on the balcony, once he was clear of the tangle of people in the center of the dance floor. "Open fire!"

"Flare!" shouted Mazzy. It was a warning only her crewmates understood, for they shielded their eyes a moment before Mazzy overloaded all the chandeliers in the room. The room went from pitch darkness to blinding light in an instant, and then the chandeliers exploded, raining crystal shards down on all of them. The goons on the balcony reeled away, yelling, and their shots went wild.

Jack was not quick enough to cover his eyes, and he

was dazzled like the rest of them. But Dad had always taught him to keep moving in a combat situation, so he kept going in the direction of the door, even though he could hardly see. Thomas slowed him down, but as much as the kid annoyed him, Jack wasn't going to leave him behind.

A few of the chandeliers had survived the overload, and though they had burned out, they still glowed faintly, enough that people could see their way dimly through the room. Boston was darting this way and that, shooting down the dazzled goons with his blaster. Dunk muscled his way to the gorilla-turtle who had met them at the door, and though he was half his size, he grabbed hold of his opponent's legs, swung him around like an Olympic hammer throw, and sent him flying into a pillar that supported the balcony overhead, smashing it to pieces. Gax's goons scrambled out of the way as a section of the balcony groaned and collapsed.

Jack had reached the doorway by now. Thomas was blubbering, fighting to catch his breath. Jack looked back, blinked tears from his eyes, and saw Ilara and

Mazzy heading their way. Blasters screamed and bolts flew through the air, but in the chaos most people were just firing wildly.

"Move it!" Jack cried.

Over their shoulders he saw one of Gax's goons spot them. This one was some kind of brightly colored slug man, carrying a long blaster rifle in his slimy appendages. He raised the rifle and took aim at Ilara.

"Look out!" Jack called, pointing.

Ilara swung around and threw out her arm toward the slug man. The creature gave a bubbling wail, and instead of firing upon them, he turned and began shooting at the other goons along the balcony. They scattered, running for cover.

"What did you do to him?" Jack asked as Ilara and Mazzy reached them.

"I showed him his worst nightmare," said Ilara with a nasty smile.

"Aaaagh! Giant pots of salt coming to get me!" the slug man screamed, his blaster blazing. "Get away!"

Most of the goons were in disarray now, but a small group of them, led by Gax, were still keeping Boston pinned down with blaster fire. Dunk lumbered over to the dumpster-sized container he had been dragging around, lifted it over his head with ease, and flung it across the length of the room at them. Gax had time for one small, pathetic squeak before it landed on him, smashing open and scattering thousands of DVDs and flash drives everywhere.

"Nooooo!" Boston howled, seeing his profit evaporate before his eyes.

"So much for *MasterChef India*," said Mazzy. "Move it, you two!"

They took to their heels then, fleeing the nightclub as blaster fire seared the gloom all around them. Out into the Underneath they went, running down alleys and dripping tunnels. Only when they were far away did they come to a halt, gasping, in the shadow of a seedy apartment complex.

Thomas sucked loudly on his inhaler. His nose was running with snot, and his eyes were full of tears. "They were trying to kill us!" he wheezed.

"That's what happens when someone puts a price on your head," said Mazzy darkly. "Question is, who did it?"

"The Hunters?" Jack suggested.

"Nah, they'd rather kill us themselves than pay someone. I think it's whoever *sent* the Hunters."

"Well, who's that?" asked Jack.

"I don't know," said Mazzy. "But I'm pretty keen on finding out."

Boston kicked an empty carton angrily. "All I wanted to do was sell trashy TV shows for a profit. Wasn't that a humble enough ambition? Instead I've ended up losing all my cargo and lumbered with two completely useless hostages, and everybody wants to kill me. What did I do to deserve this?"

"This collar you put on me is too tight," Thomas complained. "I think I'm getting a rash. I might be allergic— AAAAAAH!" He shuddered and shook as Boston electrocuted him.

"That was petty," Mazzy said. Boston had the decency to look ashamed.

Thomas shook his head, sniffed, looked around

dazedly, and sniffed again. "Wow, that thing really clears the sinuses!" he said in wonderment.

"It seems to me that we need a plan," said Ilara.

"Plan is to dump these two lumps of deadweight," said Boston, waving at Jack and Thomas. "Then we go hide in some backwater dive on the outer edges of the Nexus till everyone forgets about us."

"Solid strategy, hero," said Mazzy sarcastically. "That'll show 'em."

"I'm a Host," said Ilara, curling her lip in disdain. "I will not *hide* in some *backwater dive*."

"Look, all of you!" said Jack, holding up his hands. "I just found out my parents were androids and got orphaned in the same afternoon. There's a psycho robot, a shape-shifting slime blob, and a guy who shoots fire, all trying to kill me. And I'm sorry that I'm not whoever you thought I was and everything, but you *did* just kidnap me and Thomas from our home planet. However bad a day you're having, it's nothing compared to mine. So don't even think about dumping us here, all right? You're stuck with us for now."

Mazzy raised an eyebrow at Boston. "You do sort of owe them," she pointed out.

"I saved their lives!" he cried. "And look where it got me!"

"We're in this together now," Jack insisted. "And I've got an idea."

"Glad somebody does," Dunk muttered.

"Everyone thinks I'm this Gradius Clench superspy guy, right?" said Jack. "And they put a bounty on you because they think you're working with Gradius Clench. No one's going to believe us if we tell them otherwise. So our best bet is to—"

"Find Gradius Clench!" Thomas cried, catching on. "Yeah! I bet he can straighten things out! Maybe he and Jack can do a selfie together!"

Maybe we can, thought Jack. *And maybe then he can give me some answers, like where my real parents are.*

It was an idea that had been slowly forming ever since they'd come to Gallia. There was no point in trying to escape his kidnappers, and he wasn't sure he wanted to. Where would he go, anyway? There was nothing for him back on Earth. All he wanted now was to find the one who had caused this mess, and to make Gradius tell him who he really was.

At a stroke, he'd lost one set of parents, but he'd gained the possibility of another. What were *they* like? he wondered. Were the loving, sane parents he'd always dreamed of out there somewhere, on another planet? He needed to know.

"So let me get this straight," said Boston. "We have to find Gradius Clench to prove we have nothing to do with Gradius Clench. Any idea how we might locate him, then? You know, since half the Hunters in the galaxy have been trying to do just that for the last three years?"

"I do," said Ilara.

. . —+— . .

The Epsilon had a surprisingly dinky lounge area, with cushioned sofas to either side of a long, low table and state-of-the-art beverage makers. Boston had been forced to renovate it recently, after Dunk threatened to call his union representative because he was not getting the required quality of tea to dip his cookies in.

Jack sat on one sofa, Ilara on the other, opposite him.

Between them, Jack's sketchbook lay open. The others stood around watching. The only sound came from Thomas, who every few minutes had to snort back the runnel of snot that kept creeping out of his nose.

"Now, look at these pictures," Ilara told Jack. "Keep looking. Try to *feel* them."

"They're just sketches," Jack said. "I mean, I see the scenes in my head . . . When I was on Gallia, it was like I'd been there before . . . But I couldn't have been, right?"

"Yet somehow you *have* seen them. Somehow you knew about all these places in the Nexus, these peoples and creatures. Look at the pictures, and I will try to find their source."

Jack was uneasy about letting someone into his head, but he wasn't sure he had a choice about it.

You don't, she told him. *But it's easier if you cooperate.*

Jack sighed and started to flip through the pages. As he did, he felt himself drifting, remembering the scenes that lay before him. He saw stark deserts, plunging canyons, colorful storms on the horizon. Then he turned a page and saw the Mechanic he had drawn there, and he smelled the stink of oil and grime and sour sweat.

"Good," said Ilara. "Let yourself go." She had closed her eyes and was deep in concentration. He felt a sensation like spiderwebs brushing across his scalp. Ilara, searching his thoughts.

He turned the page and stared at the enormous burning bird. That one was not so clear as the others in his mind, but it nagged at him. What *was* it?

"These are not your memories," Ilara told him. "They are someone else's memories. Someone whose mind is linked to yours in some way."

"Gradius Clench!" Thomas cried. When the others looked at him, he shrugged. "Well, they look identical, don't they? Seems a reasonable guess."

"Indeed it does," said Ilara. "And, perhaps, if I can find the link and follow it, we might get some idea of where this person is . . . Yes . . . Yes, *there!*"

Jack's eyes widened. He felt as if he was falling backward. Everything seemed to flip and then—

He stood in a bleak white land of jagged peaks and impossibly sharp mountains, sweating in the heat of a blinding sun. Before him, towering out of the dead land like a cathedral of bones, was a temple of some kind. He saw it for only an instant before he was back in his own head again and Ilara was gazing at him, her cat eyes intense.

"Did you see anything?" Boston demanded.

"For a moment," said Ilara. "A blasted white world where nothing lived, and a temple there that looked like it was carved from some vast skeleton."

"Arcturus Prime," said Boston, grimacing.

"I was . . . I was *looking* for something," said Jack dazedly.

"If it is indeed Gradius Clench who is sharing these pictures with Jack, whatever he wants is in that temple," said Ilara.

"Then that's where we're going," said Boston. "Tool up, everybody. We're heading for the rift gate. Epsilon, get us airborne."

"Retracting ramp now."

"Without the commentary this time."

"Discontinuing commentary."

Boston waited a moment to see if his aircraft would

give him any more lip, then relaxed as he heard the engines powering up. He headed through the doorway toward the cockpit.

Mazzy slapped Jack on the shoulder. "Looks like you're part of the crew now. Welcome aboard!"

Jack felt unexpectedly warm and fuzzy at those words. "Thanks," he said. "Now, how about getting these collars off? I feel like a Labrador."

Gallia's rift gate looked a lot different from Earth's. It lay inside an enormous armored sphere that floated in the sky like a black pearl. Dozens of massive military cruisers, painted with emblems of Gallian blue and green, floated menacingly nearby like basking sharks. As the Epsilon approached, they could see traffic passing into the sphere through entrances in the side that flowed open and closed to let aircraft through, leaving a seamless reflective wall behind them.

"Why doesn't Earth have one like that?" Jack asked.

"Are you kidding?" Thomas said. He was rubbing

his newly bare neck. It turned out the collar had indeed been giving him a rash. "Can you imagine the panic if one of *those* appeared over America?"

"The rift to Earth is unstable," said Mazzy, not looking up from her console in the Epsilon's cockpit. "Every other rift exists at a fixed point and is always open. Earth's opens and closes randomly. It moves all over the world. You can't see it because it always causes a storm when it appears. Have you heard of the Bermuda Triangle?"

"That's the place just off Florida where all those planes kept mysteriously disappearing, right?" Jack said.

"Right. Except it wasn't a mystery. Most of them ended up on Moltria Rex. That seems to be where the Earth rift spits you out if you haven't given it any better instructions."

Jack gave her a sidelong glance. "Uh, instructions?"

"Yeah. There are twelve rift gates, right? All of them have a series of coordinates, like a code that gets you there. A sequence of Elder symbols. You program them into your onboard computer and *whoosh*."

139

"And there are, what, twelve of these codes?"

"Twelve that we know of. They say there are other codes, other gates out there. But without the code, you can't find the gate."

Ilara made a disdainful noise. "Rumors, that's all. There have been twelve planets in the Nexus for ten thousand years or more. If there were others, they would have been found by now."

"Ilara's just worried they'll find the thirteenth planet and it'll be full of people even more stuck up than she is," said Mazzy with a grin. Then she flinched and scowled at the elegant Host. "Hey! My childhood!" she cried. "Where'd it go?"

"You can have it back once you've said you're sorry," Ilara told her.

"I can't even remember how I got on board this aircraft!" Mazzy said, looking panicked.

"Apologize now and I might forgive you," said Ilara, studying her nails. "If you don't, I might be tempted to leave out some treasured memories."

"All right! I'm sorry!"

Ilara waved a hand. An expression of relief passed

over Mazzy's face; then it fell away, and Jack saw terrible sadness in her eyes.

"Not sure I wanted it back, after all," she muttered, and she returned to her console and didn't say another word.

Jack watched her for a moment, wondering at the source of that sadness. It felt like a cruel trick, what Ilara had done. He liked Mazzy, liked her lively, restless energy, but the Host intimidated him. He couldn't help wondering if she was reading his mind right now.

They joined a line heading into the sphere. Thomas eyed the military aircraft as they passed, bristling with turrets and cannons.

"Heavy security," he murmured. "Seems like they're very careful who they let into their gate."

"Or who they let *out*," Jack replied.

When they reached the front of the line, they found themselves facing the smooth reflective sides of the sphere, the Epsilon tiny in comparison.

"Customs checks," Boston explained. He motioned at Mazzy, whose eyes were crawling with data. "Mazzy handles all that. Even with a bounty on us, she'll run rings round their systems." A moment later, a hole opened up in the side of the sphere, the wall flowing outward as if it were made of liquid. Boston grinned. "In we go."

Jack and Thomas gawked as they saw the interior of the sphere, which they had missed on the way in, on account of being imprisoned like criminals in the hold. It was a colossal space, with lines of aircraft entering from all angles, watched over by armed drones and police vehicles. All of them were heading for the rift gate: a tightly packed, swirling ball of light in the very center of the sphere.

"That," said Thomas, "is cool."

"Arcturus Prime, here we come," said Boston, without enthusiasm.

We're on your trail, Gradius, Jack thought. *And when we find you, I want some answers about my parents.*

They flew into the rift gate. Everything stretched like a rubber band, and when it snapped back into place, they were elsewhere.

. . ✦ . .

The Epsilon sped through an empty sky over a jagged landscape of knifelike ridges and deserts of white ash. A sharp sun burned fiercely overhead. There was no water, and no birds or animals to be seen, only an endless scorching expanse with no comfort to be found.

Arcturus Prime. A tomb world, bleached clean of life by its terrible sun.

At first Jack could not stop staring at it, this alien world, but soon the unceasing whiteness became depressing. It would be many hours till they reached their destination, so Boston told them to get some sleep. Only Ilara could lead them to the temple she had seen in Jack's mind. He would wake them when they got there.

There was a bunk bed for passengers in a tiny room in the crew quarters. Jack and Thomas were shown there by Dunk, who complained the whole way that he was now a bellboy on top of everything else, and needed a pay rise.

"I call top bunk!" Thomas cried the moment the door was shut behind them. Jack shrugged and sat down slump-shouldered on the bottom bunk. He looked so gloomy that even Thomas noticed. "What's up?" he asked.

Jack didn't quite know how to explain. Everything had been moving so fast that he hadn't really had time to process it all, but as soon as they were shut in their room, it all came crashing in on him.

His parents, gone. Earth, gone. Everything he had ever known had been turned upside down, and suddenly he had been pitched into a whole new world, surrounded by strangers and beset by danger. The only piece of his past life left was Thomas, a boy he'd known barely two weeks and who'd gotten on his nerves for nearly all of it.

Thomas wiped his nose thoughtfully and adjusted his glasses, which had left a red mark. Then he plonked himself down next to Jack on the bed. "You want to talk about it?" he said.

Not really. Not with you. But he had nobody else to talk to. "I've moved so many times, you think I'd be used to it," he said. "I spent my whole time dreaming of getting away. Didn't even like my parents much.

Never thought I'd miss them, even if they were androids—"

"Wait, they were *androids*?" Thomas cried.

"Oh yeah, I didn't tell you that part yet."

"I could have sworn they were government agents," Thomas said.

"Well, they weren't."

The conversation petered out. Whatever Jack said, Thomas wouldn't get it. He didn't get anything.

"I'm all alone" was all Jack could say, and his voice cracked, and for one awful moment he thought he was going to cry.

"Hey, now! No, you're not!" Thomas said. He slung an arm around Jack's shoulders, and Jack was too dejected to resist. "You've got me, don't you? We're in this together!"

Jack sighed. Thomas was right. The last piece of Earth he had left was a chubby boy who smelled like Milk Duds and unwashed T-shirts. He might have been the most uncool boy in school, but out here it seemed like none of that mattered. Everyone from Earth was uncool as far as the rest of the Nexus was concerned. And this kid had a good heart, even if he was an infuriating goof. That meant something. Actually, it meant a lot.

"I'm glad you're here, Thomas," Jack said, and was surprised to find that he meant it.

Thomas beamed. "No problem. Us Earthers gotta stick together!"

"Yeah," said Jack. "I guess we do."

When Thomas shook Jack awake, the Epsilon's engines were quiet, and they were not moving anymore.

"We've landed," he said, his eyes massive behind the lenses of his glasses.

Jack made a noise like a bear with a blocked nose and swiped at him blearily.

Thomas dodged the blow and resumed shaking him. "You can't spend the whole day lying around! It's adventure time!"

Jack reluctantly slumped out of bed, muttering

about where he could shove his adventure time. Thomas was bouncing around like a rabbit who'd drunk too much coffee. "Come on! Come on!"

They made their way out into the gangway of the crew quarters. Nobody was around. "Epsilon?" Jack said experimentally.

"Yes, Jack?" said the computer.

"Do you know where the others are?"

"Ilara is meditating. The rest are in engineering. Shall I show you the way?" A smooth yellow line lit up on the wall, extending rapidly away from them until it turned a corner.

"Thanks!" said Jack.

"Excuse me?"

Jack hesitated, wondering if he'd done something wrong. "Er . . . I said 'thank you.'"

The Epsilon was silent for a moment. Then it gave a trembly sigh, like it was trying not to cry.

"Nobody ever says thank you to a computer," it said.

"Well, I'm from Earth," said Jack. "We have good manners."

Jack and Thomas followed the line to engineering, where they found Dunk, Boston, and Mazzy gathered together in front of a gleaming mass of coiled pipes and bizarre machinery that Jack guessed was part of the engines.

"It's the suns," said Dunk. "The Epsilon don't like all the radiation. Told you we should've got proper shielding."

"I would have, but I spent the money doing up the lounge so you could have your magnificent tea breaks," said Boston through gritted teeth.

"Union regulations say—" Dunk began to protest.

"Union regulations say you do your job and fix this engine. How long will it take?"

"Won't take long, if you give me a hand. Just need one of you to help me replace a few parts."

Boston rolled up his sleeves. "Right. Let's get on with it, then."

Mazzy noticed Jack and Thomas in the doorway. "I'm gonna take a look around, since we're here. You two want to come?"

"Yeah!" said Jack, eager to start looking for Gradius.

Thomas nodded his head so fast his glasses nearly fell off his nose.

"Sunscreen and antiradiation pills before you go outside," Boston reminded her. "And don't go into the temple till I get there."

"Yes, Dad," she said sarcastically.

"Is he really your dad?" Thomas asked in amazement as they were walking away down the corridor.

Mazzy looked at Jack. "Does he take *everything* literally?" she asked.

"More or less," Jack replied.

"Well?" Thomas asked. "Is he?"

· · ✦ · ·

They stepped off the Epsilon's ramp into a white wilderness of rock and dust. Broken columns thrust up toward a scalding yellow sky. Standing on a ridge nearby, overlooking a massive canyon, was the temple that Jack had seen in his vision. It was as white as the land that surrounded it, with sharp towers and raking spires, and just like Ilara had said, it looked as if it had been built from bones.

"Sunday church must have been a barrel of laughs," Thomas commented.

"What was Gradius Clench doing in there?" Mazzy wondered.

"More importantly, why does he look just like me, and why am I seeing in my head the places he's been?" Jack added.

"Well, yeah, that, too."

"Maybe it's *you* who looks like *him*, not the other way around?" Thomas suggested.

"Hey! If anyone's copying anyone, it's him! *I'm* an original."

Mazzy rolled her eyes. "Why don't we see if we can find him first, huh?" she said. "Then you can decide who's copying who."

The temple was not far, but it was hard going in that broken landscape. They had to clamber through narrow gaps and scrabble up slippery slopes. Before long they were sweating and gasping, their hands scratched by sharp rocks.

"Hey, Mazzy," Jack asked as they climbed. "There's something I've been wondering. I mean, you're human, right? I saw a lot of humans on Gallia, too. But humans are from Earth, aren't they? So aren't you an Earther?"

Mazzy snorted. "Not likely. It's the other way around. Humans came to Earth from elsewhere, through the rift. That's what they say, anyway. Nobody really knows. The rift gates were built while humans were still just apes or something. I guess they spread through the Nexus somehow. Some people say the Elders might have kept us as pets, like you guys do with cats." She chuckled. "Anyway, best thing about humans: We're adaptable. Slime people can't live on hot planets, and reptiles can't handle the cold, but we can live anywhere. Even a swarming disease pit like Earth!"

"How is Earth worse than *this* place?" Jack cried.

"Are you kidding? At least it's quiet here. When you're not watching ads, you're screaming at one another on the internet."

"So where are you from?" Thomas asked, pausing to gasp on his inhaler. His greasy hair was plastered to his scalp, and he looked like he was beginning to melt.

"Rakkan. The third planet."

"What's it like?" Jack asked.

"It was beautiful once," said Mazzy. "The most wonderful place in the Nexus." Her face fell. "Not anymore."

Jack took a guess. "The Mechanics?"

She nodded, her eyes glistening. She wiped away the tears before they could fall. "We were the first. They caught us by surprise. Everyone worried about the Mechanics once they appeared on Braxis Prime and took over the planet, but nobody knew what they wanted at first." Her expression became dark. "They want *everything*. The whole of the Nexus. They want to turn us all into machines like them. That's how they . . . reproduce, I suppose." She stared away into the middle distance. "That's what happened to my parents."

"Is that why there were all those military aircraft around the rift gate in Gallia?" Jack said.

Mazzy nodded. "We're wise to them now. There are only so many things that can come through a rift gate at once. If the Mechanics try to send a fleet to any of the other planets, they'll be blasted to pieces as soon

153

as they arrive." She grimaced. "But it's just a matter of time before they find some other way."

They reached the temple soon after. Up close, it was even more forbidding. Mazzy did a quick scout around the outside, but they didn't see any signs of anyone having been here.

"Who built this place?" Thomas asked, craning his neck to see up to the top.

"There was an ancient race of beings that lived here once, called the Drax. I don't know much about them, but they were terrible warriors who conquered half the Nexus before humanity's time. That was long ago. They've disappeared now."

"Gosh," said Thomas. "They certainly built scary temples, though."

Mazzy's ringtone went off, bleeping a jaunty little tune into the haunted silence. She gave them an apologetic look. "You're on speaker, Boston. What's up?"

"I'll tell you what's up! That Viper has turned up again, and it's heading right for us! The Hunters must have traced us somehow, followed us through the rift!"

"Er, that's not good," said Mazzy.

"It's the very opposite of good!" Boston yelled. "It's the other thing!"

"All right. We're heading back to the Epsilon."

"No. You'll never get here in time. We've fixed the engine, but they'll be on us in minutes. We're going to take off, try to draw them away. If we can lose them, we'll be back for you."

"You're leaving us here?" Jack cried.

"If they catch us, we're all dead. Head into the temple. We'll pick you up once we've shaken them. We're a thruster down, but we might be able to do it if we put the Epsilon into Combat Mo—"

"Did somebody say *COMBAT MODE*?" the Epsilon shrieked.

"Oh, crud," said Boston. The last thing they heard from him was a despairing howl as he was thrown across the cockpit. In the distance, the Epsilon rocketed up into the sky like a dart, engines flaring, and screamed off into the distance.

"We'd better get out of sight," Jack said.

"In *there*?" Thomas asked, eyeing the temple fearfully. He took a suck on his inhaler. This time there was no hiss when he pressed it. He tried again, to no avail. "My inhaler's run out!"

"We'll stop off at a pharmacy right after we escape the murderous psychopaths, huh?" said Jack, shoving him toward the temple.

"There they are!" said Mazzy, pointing. Over the horizon, the black bulk of the Viper was approaching fast.

They ran into the shelter of the temple, watching from an empty doorway as the Viper drew closer.

"Aren't they supposed to be following the Epsilon?" Thomas asked in a small voice.

But they weren't. They were heading straight for the temple, coming in low and fast over the peaks. Then, just as it seemed they were about to fly right over, the Viper braked hard, engines howling, blowing dust into their faces. They shrank back into the shadows as they saw a tiny figure open a door in the side of the craft and jump out, plummeting to the ground. An instant before the figure hit, rocket boots blazed into life, slowing his fall enough that he landed safely with a bump. The Viper's engines boomed, and it blazed away in the direction the Epsilon had gone.

The clouds of dust blew aside. Standing among them was a tall, thin robot in a black top hat, holding a long-barreled blunderbuss. He swept the scene with one monocled eye. TOF-1.

There, half-buried by the dust but still visible, were a set of footprints. The footprints they had left behind when they went running into the temple.

"Run," said Jack. "Inside!"

"I'm coming for you, ladies and gentlemen!" TOF-1 called as they turned tail and fled into the depths of the temple.

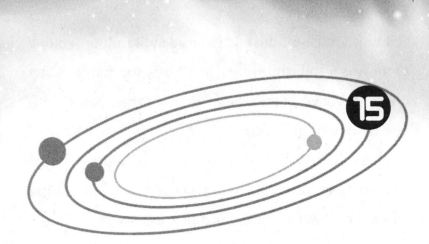

15

"If sir will please hold still for a moment so I can blast his face off?" the robot suggested politely, aiming his blunderbuss down the corridor. His monocle flared red as he unleashed a deadly bolt of energy toward Jack, and his drooping stuck-on mustache blew about crazily with the recoil.

Jack threw himself to the floor as the bolt seared past him. It exploded against the wall of the corridor, blasting out a cloud of dust and stone chips. His eyes stung and for a few seconds he couldn't see. Then he felt arms around him, pulling him up.

"What are you lying around for?" Mazzy demanded.

They staggered onward and found the end of the corridor. Thomas was already there, jigging around like he was about to wet his pants. "Come on, come on, come *on!*" he urged, beckoning frantically.

Jack looked over his shoulder, past the drifting dust that hung in the corridor. TOF-1 was striding through the sweltering gloom, his blunderbuss cradled in his hands. He wore a tweed jacket, riding breeches, and shiny black boots that clicked on the floor as he approached.

"He's crazy," Jack breathed. "Does he think he's on a fox hunt or something?"

"You really are being quite inconvenient, sir!" TOF-1 called, aiming again. An illuminated crosshairs appeared on the lens of his monocle, zooming in on Jack. Jack ducked around the corner as another sizzling energy bolt came his way.

They emerged from the corridor onto a wide balcony made of the same white stone as the rest of the temple. Stairs led down to a circular chamber. One side of the chamber was open to the outside, and through a row of arches they could see the bleached, lifeless mountains of Arcturus Prime.

In the center of the chamber was a towering statue, one side drenched in blinding light. It was a menacing robed figure, its face invisible inside a drooping hood. One of the Drax, the mysterious aliens that had built this place.

Jack and Mazzy ran down the curving steps to the floor of the chamber, overtaking Thomas, who was puffing and red-faced from far too much exercise. They had barely reached the bottom of the stairs when TOF-1 emerged on the balcony above them.

"There you are!" he said. He adjusted his top hat and sighted down the length of his blunderbuss. The crosshairs on his monocle homed in on Jack again.

"Behind the statue!" Mazzy yelled. She grabbed Jack's arm and pulled him into cover. TOF-1 blew a chunk out of the floor where Jack had been standing a moment before. Thomas tottered after them and crammed in alongside.

"What's his deal?" Jack cried, wiping sweat from his forehead with his sleeve.

"His deal?" Mazzy scanned the chamber for a way out. "His deal is, he thinks you're Gradius Clench and he's trying to kill you. Thought that was kind of obvious."

She fixed on the only exit she could see. A large metal door stood open on the far side of the chamber, flanked by two square pillars covered in alien carvings. Glowing numbers scrolled across her eyeballs as she calculated possibilities.

"Not that," said Jack. "I mean the top hat, the clothes, the snooty accent. He's a robot, not the third Lord of Winchesterhamshire!"

"Way I heard it, he was a butler once," Mazzy said. "His master was a rich man who was obsessed with those English costume dramas they used to show on Earth. *Pride and Prejudice*, that sort of thing. So he built himself a whole mansion and reprogrammed all his servants to talk like Mr. Darcy or whatever."

"Mr. Darcy never blew anyone's face off with a blunderbuss!"

"I know. Boring, right? That's why I never watch those things. Anyway, something went wrong with one of the robots. He went on a rampage, killed his master and all the other servants. He enjoyed it so much, he set himself up as a bounty hunter, just so he'd have the excuse to shoot more people. Which brings us up to now."

Jack peered out from behind the statue, then cringed back as another blast almost scalped him.

"Pinned down, sir!" TOF-1 crowed. "Nowhere to run! Surrender and I'll make it quick! An honorable death! What could be better?"

"Gee, I can't imagine," Mazzy said with a sarcastic roll of the eyes. A slobbering sound drew her attention. Thomas had his inhaler in his mouth and was sucking it desperately. "What's he doing?" she asked Jack. "I thought that thing ran out?"

"It calms him down," said Jack. "Sort of like a pacifier." He noticed the numbers scrolling across Mazzy's cybernetic eyes. "You're doing that computer-in-your-brain thing again, huh?"

"Working out our chances of escape."

"How are they looking?"

The numbers stopped scrolling as her calculations

finished. "We're doomed," said Mazzy with a shrug. Thomas sucked on his inhaler so hard his cheeks caved in.

"You always say that!" Jack accused her. "Whenever you calculate anything, it ends up as 'We're doomed!'"

"Well, I'm gonna be right eventually, aren't I?"

"Sir is going to regret it if I have to come down there!" TOF-1 warned from the balcony.

"Look, he's gonna shoot us the moment we break cover," Mazzy said. "There's no way we'll make it to that doorway. And it's only a matter of time before he figures out we don't have any weapons. Hence: doomed."

Jack cursed and kicked uselessly at the floor in frustration. "It's that stupid monocle he wears," he said. "Bet he wouldn't be such a good shot without that."

Mazzy perked up. "What do you mean?"

"There's, like, a targeting thing in it," Jack explained. "Like an electronic crosshairs. He uses it to help him aim."

Mazzy stared at him for a moment, openmouthed. "Jack," she said. "You might just have un-doomed us all."

"Awesome! Go, me!" said Jack happily. After a moment his smile turned to a puzzled frown. "Er . . . What did I do?"

"The monocle," said Mazzy, her eyes scrolling with numbers. "I'm gonna hack it."

"You're going to *hack* his *monocle*?"

"Sure. It's electronic, isn't it? If it puts out a signal, I can connect to it. And if I can connect to it, I can hack it and alter the crosshairs to make him shoot off target. Ah!" Her face cleared. "I'm in. Ten degrees to the left sound okay?"

"Sounds good to me," said Jack, who would have preferred fifty.

"Time to go, Thomas," said Mazzy. "Get that thing out of your mouth."

Thomas disengaged from his inhaler with a hiss, like a diver removing his oxygen mask. "Are you sure about this?" he asked Jack.

Jack hauled him to his feet. "I'm sure it's better than staying here."

Squeezed together behind the statue, they gazed across the space between themselves and the doorway.

Hot white light lay in stripes across the flagstones. It seemed an impossible distance to cross without getting hit.

"Last chance!" TOF-1 called. "Give up now or you have my word your deaths will be . . . unpleasant."

Mazzy slapped Jack on the shoulder. "Wanna go first?"

"No," said Jack stubbornly.

"Well, tough. It's your turn." And she shoved him out into the open.

"Aha!" brayed the robot on the balcony. He swung his blunderbuss around and put a bolt exactly ten degrees to the left of Jack's forehead.

"Run!" Mazzy shouted, and they all sprinted for the doorway as TOF-1 opened up on them, sending energy bolts here, there, and everywhere in a frenzied attempt to hit his target. Jack yelped and zigzagged as flagstones exploded around him, his hands in front of his face to protect it from flying gravel.

"Sabotage!" roared the bounty hunter. He plucked the monocle from his artificial eye and flung it aside. "Very well, you vile little grub! I shall shoot you as nature intended!"

Raising his blunderbuss, he squinted through its sights. But Jack was too quick, and with one last burst of speed he leaped through the doorway. A bolt fizzed over his shoulder, close enough that he could feel it through his clothes. Thomas tumbled past him, wheezing like a constipated balloon, and Mazzy came last, waving her hands.

"The door! Shut the door!"

TOF-1 was already hurrying down the stairs after them. Jack seized the door and tried to pull it closed, but it was made of metal and weighed a ton, and he only succeeded in making himself look desperately uncool.

"It won't close!" he yelled, still straining against it.

"There's a lever on the wall here," said Thomas from behind him. He reached out toward it. "What if I just . . ."

The door lurched forward and Jack, who had been pulling with all his might, stumbled backward and crashed to the floor. Grinding and squeaking, the door began to swing shut. From the other side, Jack heard a robotic howl of outrage. TOF-1 was at the foot of the stairs, lining up another shot.

Not fast enough. The door boomed shut a moment before they heard the scream of an energy bolt and an explosion against the metal. It was too thick to be damaged by any weapon the bounty hunter had. Jack let out a breath as he realized TOF-1 was stuck on the other side.

"Come on," said Mazzy. "We're safe for now, but it won't take him long to find a way around."

"Don't think you've gotten off scot-free, Clench!" the robot raged from beyond the door as they headed deeper into the temple. "I'll get you, that evil minx you're with, and the porky one, too! Nobody messes with a gentleman's monocle! The hunt is on!"

16

"Whoa," said Mazzy, her gaze traveling upward. "This *has* to be the place."

One by one, they stepped into the enormous hall, tiny figures in the gloomy, silent emptiness. Thin shafts of dazzling white light sliced down from slit windows high above. In the center of the room was a wide circular pedestal, a few feet high, made of black metal. There was another, much smaller pedestal nearby. At the far end were two huge statues of robed and hooded Drax, their faces hidden, hands invisible inside their oversized sleeves. Between them was a gate of the same metal as the pedestal, covered with strange writings, so large you could have sailed an aircraft carrier through it.

"Whatever Gradius was looking for, it's in here," Mazzy said confidently. "I can feel it."

"I hope so," said Jack. "'Cause I don't see any other way out, and that gate doesn't look like it's going to open anytime soon." He frowned. "Maybe we missed him," he said uncertainly. He wasn't sure he'd cope well with the disappointment if that was the case.

"Let's have a look around before we get despondent, huh?" said Mazzy. She headed straight for the central pedestal, and the others trailed after her. On closer inspection, there were panels and buttons around the edge of the pedestal. Mazzy pressed a few buttons, but nothing happened. She pressed some more, just in case.

"It's not working," Thomas observed helpfully, peering over her shoulder.

"We'll soon see about that," Mazzy said, and gave it a hefty kick. There was a hiccuping sound from inside the pedestal and then a hum of power as the machine woke up. "There!"

"Is that how you usually fix things?" Jack asked.

"Never fails," said Mazzy, limping away.

"Your toe all right?"

"Fine," she said through gritted teeth, blinking back tears.

Suddenly the chamber filled with light. They stared in amazement as constellations appeared out of the gloom. Clusters of stars speckled the air above the pedestal, with colorful gas clouds of red and green and yellow draped among them.

"Oooh!" said Thomas.

"It's a star map," Mazzy gasped, her eyes sparkling.

Jack walked around the pedestal. Scattered among the stars were planets, turning slowly in place. One was smooth and yellow-white-pinkish, a sandy desert planet; another was a lush blue green, almost completely covered in ocean.

He spotted one that looked familiar. "Hey! I think that one's Earth! I can see America!"

"The twelve planets of the Nexus," Mazzy said. "These are the planets that the Elders placed rift gates on to connect them together."

"What's that little symbol floating next to Earth?" Jack asked, pointing to a small red sign that looked like an angry Space Invader.

"Pretty sure that's the intergalactic symbol for cooties," Mazzy said.

"Earth does *not* have cooties!" Jack said, offended.

Mazzy shrugged. "Symbol says different. Face it, you've been quarantined for so long that even an extinct alien race didn't want to visit."

Jack grumbled sourly as he trudged around the star map. He wasn't even particularly fond of Earth, but he still felt the need to defend it. It was his home, after all. His and Thomas's. It got on his nerves that everyone thought they were hicks from some backwater fleapit.

"You said there were twelve planets in the Nexus, right?" Thomas asked.

"Yep," said Mazzy.

"I count thirteen."

Mazzy looked again. "You're right!" she said, counting the planets. "There's Gallia . . . there's Akkaris . . . Moltria Rex . . ." She paused, peering at a large, colorful planet with many moons and wide rings around it, like a blue-and-purple Saturn. It turned beneath the light of two suns. "So where's *that?*"

"Maybe that's what Gradius was looking for," Jack suggested, getting excited. "Maybe it's the homeworld of the Drax!"

"A lost planet!" Mazzy grinned. "There've always been rumors that there are more rift gates out there, connections to other planets that broke down or were forgotten thousands of years ago. If Gradius isn't here, I'll bet he's headed there."

"Can we go after him?" Jack asked eagerly.

"Sure! Once we have the coordinates, we ought to be able to get there through any rift gate." She squinted. "I'm gonna need to download the data, though. Let me see what I can do."

Her eyes began to scroll with code again. Thomas grew bored and wandered off through the baking heat and shadow, toward the massive gate. Jack let him go, content to stare in wonder at the stars that hung in the air above him.

Not long ago, he'd despaired of ever leaving his small, dull town. Now he had a whole galaxy to roam.

He thought of his sort-of friends he'd left behind. They had no idea of what was out here. They would be sitting down to class right about now, while he was adventuring in space.

A little smile spread across his face. Homicidal robots aside, this whole thing was actually pretty cool.

"Hey, look! I found something!" Thomas called. Jack looked over. Thomas was standing in front of a panel of shiny black stone, set into the wall near the huge gate. He touched his finger to it, and a little symbol appeared there, glowing white. He touched elsewhere, and another symbol appeared. He dragged it across the stone with his finger to join the first one, and they both changed shape and turned green.

"It's like a puzzle or something!" Thomas said, beaming. "I like puzzles!"

"Why does he always have to mess with everything?" Mazzy sighed.

Jack made an *I dunno* face. "Keeps him happy, I guess."

"Oh!" Mazzy blinked and raised her head as they heard the hum of something powering up. "Wait! I think I just did something!"

"Indeed you did!" intoned a deep voice from behind them. They both yelped and spun around. Standing on the smaller pedestal was a sinister robed figure, its face covered by a heavy hood. "Who dares intrude on the forbidden sanctum of the Drax?"

Jack wasn't quite sure how to respond to that. "Er . . . me!" he said uncertainly. Then he thumbed at Mazzy. "And her."

"And me!" Thomas squeaked from the far side of the hall.

"Oh," said the hooded figure. "Okay, then. Um . . . Welcome!"

"Thanks. Are you a hologram?" Jack stepped closer and waved a hand through the figure's legs.

"Don't do that! I'm an artificially intelligent projected entity, actually."

"Hologram," Mazzy said wisely.

"Look, what do you want?" the hooded figure asked, getting annoyed. "Do you have any questions? That's why I'm here, to answer questions. It's sort of my reason for existing. I don't know why you activated me otherwise."

Jack thought for a moment. "Yeah, I do have a question. What happened to everyone?"

"Ah! That *is* a good question." The hologram regained its dignity now that it was back on familiar ground, and its voice deepened. "You stand in a temple built by the Drax, ancient wanderers among the stars! Their empire existed long ago, back when you humans were just a bunch of fish with big ideas. Once they ruled half the Nexus! But there was one thing they could never conquer."

"The other half?" Jack suggested.

Somehow the hologram managed to give him an irritated glance even through its hood. "I speak of Death itself!" it boomed, raising its arms to reveal black-gloved hands. "The Drax realized they would never be truly free until they could live forever. For a thousand years the greatest minds of the empire struggled with the problem. Then came Gttht the Persuasive."

"Gttht?" Jack tried to pronounce it the way the hologram had. It made his tongue itch.

"Gttht! Emphasis on the second *t*."

"GtTTTht!" Jack tried again, but only ended up

spluttering all over Mazzy. She flinched and wiped away a mist of spittle from her cheek.

"Ew! Just call him the Persuasive, okay? Anyway, so what did Gt . . . Mr. Persuasive do?"

"Gttht knew of one being in all the galaxy that never aged and never died. The million-year-old Fangbeast of Arcturus Prime. So he persuaded our finest minds to build a temple here so that we might worship the Fangbeast and it could teach us the secret of its immortality."

"Uh-huh," said Mazzy. "Worship the Fangbeast. How did that work out for you?"

"Not well. It was, er, more interested in eating us, actually. In fact it ate almost everybody."

"When you say *finest minds*," said Jack, "how fine are we talking?"

"Guys! I get it now!" Thomas cried suddenly from the other side of the hall, where he was still playing with the glowing symbols on the black stone panel. "It's kind of like Sudoku!"

"What's he doing over there?" The hologram craned to see.

"Never mind him; he's relatively harmless," said Mazzy. "Hey, why do you all wear hoods?"

"What?"

"It's just occurred to me. Every statue in here is wearing a hood. Why do you hide your faces?"

"Because our faces are so terrible, so frightening, that the merest glimpse of them would send you screaming in—"

"I wanna see!" Mazzy said eagerly. "Take off your hood!"

"No," the hologram said, pouting.

"Go on. You've got nothing to lose. Your whole race is extinct; there's no one left to care."

"That was a bit uncalled for," the hologram complained. Then it sighed. "Oh, very well. Don't say you weren't warned, though. Behold the dreadful Drax!" With a dramatic sweep, the hologram threw back its hood.

Jack and Mazzy stared at the creature revealed beneath. Huge soft eyes gazed out of a furry, whiskered face. Floppy ears hung to either side, and a little pink nose twitched and sniffed.

"Aww!" said Jack. "Cute! You look kind of like a bunny rabbit!"

"No!" the hologram cried. "We are the Drax! Scourge of the Red Nebula! Destroyers of the Idikan Empire! Seekers of Forbidden Knowledge!"

"Adorbs!" Mazzy agreed. "You're just a bunch of sweetie snuffle bunnies, aren't you?"

The hologram sagged. "See, this is why we wear hoods. It's not easy ruling half a galaxy when no one takes you seriously. We'd meet with enemy leaders to negotiate, and they'd keep trying to pet us."

Mazzy quickly drew back her hand, which had been reaching out to scratch the hologram behind the ear. "So, er, what happened to the Fangbeast?" she asked.

"In the end, we summoned our bravest warriors to battle the monster, and they succeeded in imprisoning it in this very temple. Then we retreated back through the rift gate in shame. All our greatest minds had been eaten. Our empire sort of fell apart after that, and the way to our homeworld was forgotten."

"You imprisoned it . . . in this very temple, you

say?" Jack was suddenly wary. "And it's a creature that lives forever?"

"Yes, but fear not!" said the hologram. "Its prison was secured with a lock so fiendish that not even the cleverest Drax could hope to undo it."

"Oh. That's all right, then."

"Yet there was one last thing. Before he died of his wounds, Gttht the Persuasive made a prophecy. In one hundred thousand years, he said, a mighty hero would appear, whose genius was so great that they would solve the impossible riddle and release the awful Fangbeast once again!"

Jack looked uncertainly at Thomas, who was still fiddling with the puzzle at the end of the hall. "Er . . . And how long has it been since that prophecy was made?"

"Let me check my data banks," said the hologram. Its ears lifted in surprise. "Well, what are the chances? It was exactly one hundred thousand years ag—"

There was a small *ding*, as if an elevator had just arrived. "Solved it!" Thomas declared proudly.

Mazzy, Jack, and the hologram looked at one another as it dawned on them what had just happened.

"Well, my work here is done!" said the hologram with nervous haste. "Farewell and good luck!" And it disappeared.

Mazzy and Jack turned deadly glares onto Thomas. "What?" asked Thomas.

There was a loud screeching noise as the enormous gate began to slide open behind him.

"Why do you have to mess with everything?!" Jack shouted, waving his hands about angrily.

"I can't help it! I have an inquiring personality!" Thomas shouted back, waving his hands, too.

"Boys, instead of yelling at each other, how about we leave now?" Mazzy suggested, pointing up the corridor they had come from.

"Uh-uh! You won't be going anywhere!" came the reply. From the shadows of the corridor, TOF-1 stepped into view, his blunderbuss slung over his shoulder. "I heard you all the way across the temple. Silence is a virtue you'd do well to learn."

He moved unhurriedly into the chamber. There was no way past him, and he knew it.

"Now, who wants to get shot first?" he wondered.

Jack turned and looked as the enormous gate clanged to a halt, now fully open. Beyond, the darkness was total.

He heard a rattling growl, low and loud enough to make the room rumble. In the blackness, two huge eyes opened, each as big as Jack was, containing two hourglass-shaped pupils. Directly above them, another pair of eyes opened. And another pair above that.

TOF-1 on one side. The Fangbeast on the other.

"Told you," Mazzy said in a small voice. "Doomed."

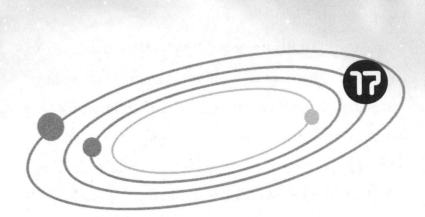

Thomas stared at the monster as it emerged, his mouth in an O, making a squealing noise so high-pitched it would have been audible only to bats and two-year-olds. The Fangbeast was the size of a building, six horrible eyes piled on top of an enormous mouth with teeth as big as lampposts. It waddled on six stumpy legs, somewhat like a leathery frog, if that frog had Godzilla for a dad. A long, thick tail snaked out behind it, ending in a knobbed club the size of a phone booth.

"What, what?" TOF-1 cried as he laid eyes on it. "Can it be? The Fangbeast of Arcturus Prime?"

The Hunter's attention had been captured by the hideous creature. Jack caught Mazzy's eye and thumbed urgently toward the side of the room. The two of them scampered out of the Fangbeast's way. A moment later, Jack returned, and dragged Thomas—still squealing—off toward the side of the enormous chamber.

TOF-1 was busy cranking up the power on his blunderbuss, his gaze fixed on the Fangbeast as it came thumping out from between the two massive hooded statues that flanked the gate. "The Fangbeast, by Jingo! The ultimate prize for the big game hunter! Oh, won't the folks back at the club go green with envy when they see *this* on my wall!"

"He is actually crazy," whispered Jack in amazement.

"Never mind that," Mazzy said. "Try to get around behind him. We need to get out while he's busy."

Jack's reply was cut short by an earsplitting bellow that shook the room, and the Fangbeast broke into a charge, thundering across the chamber toward TOF-1, who was at the far end. TOF-1, having finished preparing his gun, was absolutely calm in the face of the onrushing monster. He cocked his top hat jauntily and raised his blunderbuss to his eye.

"Maximum power, old boy," he said. "Night night."

A bolt of energy screamed forth from the end of the blunderbuss, flew across the chamber, and struck the Fangbeast in the spot directly between all six of its eyes.

The Fangbeast didn't even slow down.

"Ah," said TOF-1. "My mistake."

The Fangbeast's huge jaws slammed shut on him and crunched him down. Then it turned its many eyes toward the three remaining morsels that cowered against the wall nearby.

"Run?" Jack suggested in a tiny voice.

"Run," Mazzy agreed.

They fled in different directions, driven by blind panic. The Fangbeast swept its club-like tail through the air and brought it down toward Jack, but years of training with his dad had made him fast, and he darted out of the way. It smashed into the floor behind him, sending flagstones flying. He raced for cover, searching for something to hide behind, but the chamber was almost bare except for the pedestal in the center, where the cowardly hologram had stood. Frantically he looked for a way to get around the Fangbeast, back through the doorway that would lead to the outside, but the creature was just too big.

It turned its attention to Thomas. Thomas, who was standing in the corner, frozen like a mouse caught in a cat's gaze. He trembled as its six eyes fixed on him, one by one, and it gave a low snarl like the rumbling of a distant earthquake.

The Fangbeast walked toward him with the slow confidence of a predator that knows its prey is caught. Mazzy tugged on Jack's arm and pointed. Now that the Fangbeast had moved, the way out of the chamber was clear.

But Jack couldn't tear his eyes away from Thomas. He was waiting for him to make a break for it, to run and hide, to do *something*. Instead he was just standing there, sniffling. Jack realized that he wasn't going to move. The sight of the monster had paralyzed him with fright.

If Jack ran, Thomas would be next on the menu. He

couldn't let that happen. Thomas was a pest, but he was *Jack's* pest. And . . . well . . . Jack had sort of grown used to him by now. He kind of liked having him around, in fact.

So he cupped his hands to his mouth and hollered, "Hey! Over here!"

The Fangbeast swung around and glared at Jack and Mazzy.

"What are you *doing?*" Mazzy squealed through gritted teeth.

Jack was wondering that himself, but it seemed too late to back out of it now. "Yeah, I'm talking to you!" Jack yelled at the beast. "Try picking on someone your own size!"

"There *is* no one its own size," Mazzy pointed out, doing her best not to be noticed as she shuffled away from Jack.

The Fangbeast roared, sensing defiance from its tiny prey. It wasn't used to people shouting at it.

Jack flinched as he was hit by a wave of stinking breath. "And get some mouthwash down you as well! You smell like a pile of dead otters!"

Whether it was the tone of his voice or the unlikely misfortune that the creature could understand English, that was too much. The beast roared again, and its tail lashed out. Jack flung himself to the ground as the crushing weight of it passed over his head, smashing into the wall behind him. Light flooded in from outside as the wall broke into pieces. Jack covered his head with his hands and scrunched himself up as small as he could as huge chunks of rubble rained down all around him.

Why didn't I keep my big mouth shut? he asked himself frantically. *Why, why, why?*

But the pounding of falling stone petered out, and he raised his head, amazed to find himself still unhurt. Behind him, the wall to the chamber had mostly fallen away. Beyond was a cliff edge, plunging thousands of feet down to a scorched canyon below.

The Fangbeast glared at him and bared its considerable teeth.

"Uh-oh," Jack muttered, sensing its intention.

Then it bellowed and charged.

Jack had nowhere to go. There was no way he could

187

dodge something that size. Behind him was a fatal fall. All he could do was stand where he was, his pupils shrinking as he saw the end bearing down on him. All he could think of for his final word was: *Oops*. It would make for a very small gravestone.

Then, from behind and below, a howl of engines. Wind blasted around him, making him stagger forward. He turned, a grin spreading on his face, expecting to see the Epsilon there, Boston Sark arriving for a last-minute save.

It wasn't the Epsilon. It was a small, light aircraft, looking something like a helicopter gunship, and crouched in its cockpit Jack saw . . .

Himself.

The pilot pressed his thumb down on a button. Rockets streaked out from under the gunship's wings, screeching past Jack. They smashed into the Fangbeast, one, two, five, *ten* of them, a cascade of explosions that made Jack cringe and cover his face. The creature disappeared in a cloud of black smoke and flame.

"Get in!" cried a voice over the gunship's loudspeaker system. Gradius Clench swung the aircraft closer, and a door to the cargo hold opened in its side. "Jump!"

"He sounds just like you!" Mazzy told Jack as she sprinted past and leaped out into the sky, clearing the gap with ease to tumble into the back of the gunship.

"I do *not* sound like that!" Jack yelled at her.

"Everyone says that when they hear their own voice! Now jump!"

Jack looked back at the steadily clearing cloud of smoke. Still no sign of Thomas.

"Jump!" Gradius urged him.

Jack cursed under his breath and ran into the smoke.

Where is he? Where is he? he thought. Something vast moved in the murk, the shifting of an enormous flank. Jack realized that the Fangbeast was not dead, was still standing, in fact. At any moment an enormous foot might descend through the smoke to stamp him flat, or a huge tail might swat him into next week. His heart pounded as he fought the urge to abandon Thomas to his fate. It was Thomas who'd activated the distress beacon, after all. Thomas's fault his parents had died. Thomas's fault he was being hunted.

And it was Thomas's fault he'd been torn from a dull life of exhausting work and constant tests and thrown into a world of adventure in the Nexus, the place he'd dreamed about all his life. That meant Jack owed him. Owed him big.

He heard a hacking cough, the helpless wheeze of the sick-note kid. Thomas's asthma was a beacon, leading Jack through the smoke. He stumbled in that direction, coughing into his fist, and bumped into something soft and pudgy that was definitely not a Fangbeast.

Thomas clutched on to him. "Jack! Jack! Get me out of here!" he sniffled in blind panic.

"What do you think I'm trying to do?" Jack cried. He grabbed hold of Thomas and pulled him into motion, dragging him in the direction of the sunlight, which he could just about make out through the thin-

ning smoke.

Something huge moved across the sun, blocking it out. The Fangbeast, its head swinging restlessly here and there. Looking for them.

"Keep going!" Jack muttered as Thomas's legs threatened to wobble again. He steered them around the Fangbeast, which had mercifully not spotted them yet. The Fangbeast's club tail swung through the air, stirring the haze as it passed overhead, making them both duck. By now there was hardly any smoke left, and they could see the beast towering over them, and Gradius's gunship still hovered uneasily just beyond the broken wall.

Jack slapped Thomas on the shoulder. "Go!"

Thomas was really not fast. He was the kind of kid you dreaded getting on your team in gym class. He waddled and puffed and snorted at such a lamentable pace that Jack wondered if he'd forgotten he was supposed to be running for his life. Jack could have cleared the distance with ease, but he had to lag back to keep level with Thomas.

The Fangbeast spotted them before they'd even made it halfway. Its rubbery lips skinned back over its teeth.

"It's seen you! Move it!" cried Gradius through the loudspeaker. He opened up the gunship's blasters, sending a volley of plasma fire into the monster, but though it roared in pain, the shots did little more than distract it.

"We're going to jump!" Jack told Thomas as Gradius turned the gunship side-on again and moved in as close as he dared.

"I can't!" Thomas wailed, eyeing the gap between the ledge and the gaping door of the gunship, where Mazzy waited, holding out her hand.

"You can!" Jack told him, one hand on his collar, propelling him onward. "You can do it!"

The Fangbeast blinked as it shrugged off the effects of Gradius's last attack and turned its attention back to its fleeing prey. Angrily, it broke into a run.

"Ready?" Jack cried as they neared the edge.

"No!" Thomas blubbered.

The ground shook as the monster pounded toward them, closing the distance in moments.

"Jump!" Jack shouted.

The two of them leaped out into the air, flailing. For an instant Jack saw the terrifying drop pass beneath him. Then his feet hit the floor, and he tumbled into the cargo hold among the crates and piles of tarp. The moment he was inside, the gunship lurched upward and away. He caught a glimpse of the Fangbeast, jaws wide, pounding closer. He saw it bunch its many legs and leap—

Then the gunship rocketed forward, and the Fangbeast missed them. Jack scrambled to the doorway and looked out in time to see it plummeting through the air toward the ground, far, far below.

"He'd better hope he really *is* immortal," Jack muttered. There was a tiny *paf* and a small puff of smoke as the monster hit the ground. Jack rolled his shoulders and looked back inside the gunship. "Everyone all right?"

"Mmmmf," said Mazzy, who was lying pinned underneath Thomas, her arms and legs waving helplessly. Thomas himself had fainted.

"See?" Jack said to him. "Told you you could jump."

The cockpit was sealed off from the gunship's cargo hold, so they were unable to speak to Gradius after he had rescued them. The burning white landscape sped by below, visible through the open door in the side of the aircraft, and they were surrounded by the sound of the engines. Hot wind stirred their hair as they picked themselves back up after their encounter with the Fangbeast.

Jack helped Mazzy extract herself, red-faced and angry, from beneath the unconscious Thomas. After she was free, she volunteered to help wake him up by giving him a few slaps around the face. Jack said he'd wake him instead. Mazzy looked a bit too eager.

A little gentle shaking had Thomas back with them. Once he came to terms with the fact that he was still alive, he crawled over to a corner and sat there looking ashamed.

"Sorry," he mumbled at last.

"What for?" Jack asked.

"I . . . I guess I just froze up. That thing just scared me so much."

"You weren't much use in the nightclub, either," Mazzy reminded him.

Jack gave her a look. "We're not all cut out to be action heroes, okay?" he told her.

"No. Some of us are just here to screw things up and slow everyone down," said Thomas miserably. "You both nearly got killed because of me."

Jack began to argue, then realized that he really couldn't. "Yeah, well," he said. "We're all still here, though, aren't we?"

That didn't seem to make Thomas feel much better, so Jack went over and sat next to him. "Hey," he said.

"Come on. We just escaped certain death at the hands of a three-story-tall monster. What else were you going to do with your Saturday?"

Thomas looked even more glum. "I was going to spend it on my own, like always," he said. "You were supposed to come for a sleepover, but you went off with Jodie Ellis instead."

Mazzy raised an eyebrow. "Jodie Ellis, eh?"

"She turned out to be a slime creature," said Jack. "Long story."

"You think I don't know what everyone thinks of me?" Thomas said. "I'm a klutz. I'm a goof. I say the wrong thing all the time. No wonder everyone tries to avoid me or pretend I'm not there. I know you want to get rid of me, just like Mom did."

Jack was shocked by that. "Hey, hey! Your mom did *not* want to get rid of you!"

"How would you know? You never asked about her. All she did was watch TV. She could go days without saying a word to me."

Jack's stomach plummeted, and he felt utterly awful. Thomas was right: Jack had never been interested enough to ask. No wonder he was so desperate for attention that he'd latch on to anyone who would give it to him. All this time Jack had been complaining about how hard it was for him, with his weird parents and their assault courses, when Thomas had it much worse and would have traded places with him in an instant. He could hardly imagine what it must have been like to be so *ignored*.

"Oh, man," he said. "It's not you who should be sorry; it's me."

Thomas shrugged.

"Anyway . . ." said Jack, struggling to find a way to make it up. "Anyway, you're wrong."

"Wrong about what?"

"I don't care if you're a goof. *I'm* a goof, too. I'm not really any good at anything, except that I can draw a little. And where do you think all *my* friends are? I've never had any that lasted more than a year, because I always had to leave them behind."

"Are you seriously having a contest to see who's the most unpopular?" Mazzy asked in amazement.

Jack ignored her. "Listen, Thomas. You know how

197

many people ever bought me a birthday cake? Zero. You know what I'd be doing right now if it weren't for you? I'd be doing Dad's assault course again, still wondering why my parents were so weird, waiting for the next time we moved so I could lose all my friends and start over. So I *don't* want to get rid of you. If I did, I'd have left you in that temple. I want you to stick with me. Nobody else ever has."

That finally got a smile out of Thomas, and he seemed to buck up a little. "All right," he said. "Yeah, I can do that."

Mazzy rolled her eyes. "You two are something, you know that? What a pair. Is everyone from Earth like you?"

Jack grinned. "Only the awesome ones," he said.

. ∘ ✦ ∘ .

A short distance from the temple was a cavern inside a mountain. Gradius steered the gunship in through a cleft in the rock and put them down on a ledge high up on the cavern's side. Beams of blinding sunlight lanced down through the gloom from gaps overhead, illuminating a landscape of strange and colorful rock formations and delicate, glittering crystal flowers. The suns had bleached all life and color from the surface, but here in the shade, there grew a hard kind of beauty.

They climbed out and found him waiting there, his back to them, looking thoughtfully over the lip of the ledge into the echoing space below. He turned around as his passengers emerged and gave them a steady gaze.

Jack studied him uneasily. Now that they were face-to-face, he felt a little afraid. He wondered if Gradius really had the answers he was seeking and whether he'd like what he heard if he did.

It was like looking into a mirror and seeing a more handsome version of himself. Gradius's features were identical, but he stood straighter, with a certain self-assuredness that Jack lacked. Plus he had a better haircut. Jack didn't generally like to see photos of himself, but every once in a while a picture caught his best side. The boy before him seemed to be made up of best sides. There wasn't a bad angle to him.

"So, which one are you?" he asked Jack.

Jack was puzzled by the question. "I'm Jack," he said. "From Earth."

"And you're Gradius Clench," Mazzy said.

He favored her with an easy smile. Jack was appalled and faintly jealous to see Mazzy smile back.

"That's me," he said. "So, you mind telling me what you were doing in an old Drax temple on Arcturus Prime?"

"We were looking for you," said Mazzy.

"I'm flattered," said Gradius. "Well, now you've found me. Why don't you tell me why you were looking?"

"Before we get into all that, there's the matter of Boston and the others," said Mazzy. "They could still be in trouble."

"If they are, we can't help them now," said Gradius. "I'm sorry, but they're on their own. I can't risk exposing myself to those Hunters. There's too much on the line." Mazzy took a breath to argue, but Gradius gestured toward the gunship. "They have a military-grade combat aircraft. Mine's built for stealth. I can't fight them in that."

"But we need to do *something*!" Mazzy cried.

"If they spot us, they'll shoot us out of the sky. And the mission I'm on . . . well, let's just say the fate of the Nexus might depend on it. So I'd rather not die yet, and I'd rather you all didn't, either. We'll simply have to trust they can get out of it themselves."

Mazzy looked frustrated, but she seemed to accept that he was right. Thomas blundered forward and thrust out a hand. "I'm Thomas!" he said enthusiastically.

Gradius pumped his hand. "Great to meet you, Thomas," he said, and sounded like he meant it. Jack hated how smooth he was. He had a way of making people like him. Jack didn't have that skill. "Now, I bet you're the guy to fill me in on how you all got here," he told Thomas.

Thomas eagerly obliged, delivering a breathless recap of events so far, which only ended when he got to the part about Mazzy activating the mysterious pedestal in the temple.

"You managed to make it work?" Gradius asked Mazzy. "Incredible! How did you do it?"

Mazzy waved it away modestly. "Oh, just takes a bit of mechanical know-how," she said.

"She kicked it," Jack told him.

"I'd never have thought of that," he said with admiration. "I was trying to get the pedestal to work when my gunship detected your approach, so I retreated to a safe distance to see if you were friend or foe. What did you find when you turned it on?"

"A star map!" said Thomas. "And we found the coordinates for a rift gate on—"

"The thirteenth planet!" Gradius said excitedly. "You have them with you?"

"Right here," said Mazzy, tapping her head.

"That's what I came for!" said Gradius. "Come over to the gunship! All you have to do is transfer them into the onboard computer and—"

"Uh-uh," said Mazzy, shaking her head, her multicolored locks flopping around. "Not until you give us some answers."

"But it's critical to the safety of the Nexus that I get to the thirteenth planet!"

"Oh yeah?" said Mazzy. "Why?"

"That," said Gradius with a charming wink and a flourish, "is classified."

Mazzy was not impressed. "Then so are the coordinates."

Jack was pleased to see irritation flash across the superspy's annoyingly handsome face. "Did I mention it was critical to the safety of the Nexus?"

"Three of my friends are out there being chased by bounty hunters, and we all nearly got killed by a psycho robot with class issues," Mazzy said. "All because everyone thinks Jack here is you. I figure you owe us an explanation, don't you? You can start by telling us why you two look freakily alike."

Gradius looked at Jack, surprised. "Nobody told you yet? Not even your Guardians?"

"My . . . *Guardians* are dead," said Jack. "Until about twenty-four hours ago, I thought they were my parents."

"Oh," said Gradius, his eyes softening in sympathy. "I can see how you might be confused, then."

"I am, a little," Jack said dryly. "And I'd really like to know what happened to my *real* parents, too."

A strange expression flickered across Gradius's face, something that might have been sadness. He turned away and looked out over the cavern, his hands linked behind his back, while he tried to think where to begin. Jack watched him, framed against the beams of light slanting down from the roof. His very existence made Jack feel inadequate. He was just more . . . *heroic* somehow. Even the way he stood was heroic. His parents . . . his *Guardians* had wanted him to be like that—strong, confident, and proud—but he'd never managed to live up to their expectations.

"There is a secret organization called the Hexagram," Gradius said at last. "They work behind the scenes, looking out for the good of the Nexus. They don't follow any law but their own. They don't recognize any government. They just do whatever needs to be done to keep us all safe." His voice became dark. "*Whatever* needs to be done."

Thomas squealed with delighted excitement, clapping his hands together. Jack gave him a look.

"They saw the Mechanics coming long before anyone else did," Gradius continued. "They warned people, but nobody listened. They tried to stop it, but they couldn't. So they made plans to deal with the Mechanics when the time came. One of those plans was us."

"Us?" said Jack.

"Him?" said Mazzy in surprise, pointing at Jack.

"The idea was to create a superspy who could infiltrate the Mechanics. Someone nobody would suspect. A kid. And not only that, but a kid who could come back from the dead."

"You can come *back from the dead*?" Thomas gawked at Jack.

"I don't know, and I am totally not finding out," said Jack. "What are you talking about, Gradius?"

"I'm talking about clones," he said. "There were ten of us born, all identical in every way. Ten of us sent to ten different planets in the Nexus. The idea was—"

"Wait!" said Jack, who couldn't bear not knowing a moment longer. "Born to *whom*? If my Guardians weren't my parents, who were?"

Gradius gave him a pitying gaze. Jack felt a sense of dread settle on him, and he knew the answer before Gradius gave it.

"We don't have any parents," said Gradius. "We were grown in a tank."

"Cool!" Thomas breathed, completely missing the stricken look on Jack's face.

Jack went numb. In the space of less than a day he'd lost two sets of parents: one fake, and one imaginary. Now there was nothing left to hold on to. His Guardians were the only parents he would ever have, and there was no one to replace them. He felt that loss at last, sudden and hard, like a punch in the guts.

They're gone. They're really gone.

Gradius went on, a little more gently. "The idea was that we would all be intensively trained from birth, and when the time came, the best of us would be sent into action. The rest would be kept on standby. If the one who was in action got killed, the next one would step in and take his place. His friends and contacts would think he'd miraculously escaped death, and the legend of Gradius Clench would grow. His enemies would think he actually *was* dead, so they'd never see it coming when the next one turned up. As far as anyone knew, there was only ever one Gradius Clench. But really, there were ten."

"The ultimate spy!" Thomas gasped, his enormous eyes sparkling. "Every time you think you've killed him, he keeps coming back!"

"And which one are you?" Mazzy asked.

"I'm number two."

"Wait, wait!" Jack waved his hands in front of Gradius's face, swinging from sadness to anger in an instant. "You're saying I'm an *insurance policy?*"

"More like a spare, actually," said Gradius. "Anyway, I wouldn't worry. If I die, the honor of being Gradius Clench passes on to the next-most-competent clone. I've read your progress reports. If there's a list some-where, I'm pretty sure you're at the bottom of it."

He gave Jack a pat on the shoulder, which was meant to be comforting but made him seethe instead. The very sight of Gradius made his blood boil. Here was a boy who was the embodiment of everything his dad had ever wanted. Jack paled in comparison to him. He knew it wasn't entirely fair, but fury felt better than anguish.

Mom. Dad. You weren't much, but you were my safe place, even so. Now nowhere is safe anymore.

"If you're a superspy, how come everyone knows your face?" Thomas asked Gradius, oblivious to the turmoil Jack felt. "I mean, it's all over the space news, or whatever you call it out here."

Gradius looked grave. "We don't know. My predecessor was doing great work sabotaging the Mechanics' plans, even though he had to tread on the toes of a lot of powerful people to do it. He was on the verge of finding a way to shut them down for good. Then something went wrong. A leak inside the Hexagram, maybe. Someone tipped off the Mechanics, and General Kara ambushed him. That's why I was activated."

Mazzy had gone pale. "General Kara?" she said.

"Yes. And since then three more of our clones have gone missing. I'd assumed you were safe on Earth, Jack, since it's literally the last place anyone would want to go to look for anything—"

"Hey!"

"But then you sent that distress signal, which you're

only supposed to send if your cover is blown and you're in deadly peril."

Thomas looked sheepish and studied his toes.

"Well, whoever leaked our face to the world must have also given General Kara the key to decode our messages, because she knew right away that it had come from you, and the next time the rift gate to Earth opened, she sent those Hunters through. You're lucky this young lady and her people got to you first."

Lucky, thought Jack bitterly. *Luckier still if Thomas had never come by on my birthday and found the attic.*

But was that true? Would he have rather stayed in the life he had, instead of a new life of adventure on alien planets? He couldn't blame Thomas for what had happened; only a moment ago he'd been thanking him for it. And yet now that there was no prospect of finding his parents, he felt lost, directionless. The anger drained out of him and left him empty. They'd found Gradius, and he had no answers. What was he doing here, then?

Gradius turned to Mazzy, out of patience. "Now, listen. I've told you what I know. You need to give me those coordinates. My predecessor found out the

Mechanics are cooking up something big. I've been trying to find out what, but you can bet it won't be good for us. All I've got so far are rumors that they've found the thirteenth planet and they're up to something there. That, and the name they've given to their plan. *Firehawk.*"

Firehawk. Jack's mind went back to the picture in his sketchbook. A flaming bird, flying through space.

"So you want to go to this mysterious thirteenth planet to find out what the Mechanics are up to and what this Firehawk thing is?" Mazzy said.

"Yes!"

"All right," said Mazzy. "Let's go."

"Er," said Gradius. "No, I just meant me."

"You're going up against General Kara?" Mazzy said fiercely. "Then I'm coming. It was her who led the invasion against my planet, against her *own people.* Her fault my parents were enslaved. You're not leaving me behind!"

"Me, either!" said Thomas eagerly.

They all looked at Jack, and in that moment Jack realized what he needed to do. Mom and Dad had trained him for this. His whole purpose in life was to be some sort of hero, even if he was terrible at it. To turn away from that would be letting them both down, and he wouldn't do that. He couldn't. Androids or not, they'd raised him and given their lives for him. He had to make that sacrifice worth something.

"I'm in," he said firmly.

"Look, I appreciate the enthusiasm, but this is all wrong," said Gradius. "I work alone. I can't be dragging you three around with me. We're going into the heart of enemy territory. Do you know how dangerous it will b—"

"Yadda, yadda, yadda," said Mazzy, making a blah-blah duck beak with her hand. "I have the coordinates. If you want to go through that rift gate, you take us with you. End of discussion."

Gradius stared at her in amazement, then looked at Jack. "Is she always like this?" he asked.

"Mostly," said Jack.

Gradius sighed. "Then I suppose I have no choice. Come on, then. Into the gunship."

"*Yesss!*" said Thomas, fist-pumping the air.

Going through a rift gate felt unpleasantly like being put through a pasta maker. Jack felt himself squashed and squeezed, and the very air around him seemed to stretch. Then everything snapped back into place, and there was just the three of them in the back of the gunship, with the lights down dim and the engines humming all around them.

"Are we there yet?" Thomas asked, looking slightly nauseous.

"Why don't we find out?" said Jack, and he pulled

open the sliding door in the side of the aircraft and looked out over a new world.

In the distance, colossal four-winged birds flapped their way through velvet evening skies. Below them lay a sprawling, cracked land of canyons and gorges, where forests of colorful, alien trees covered the mountainsides. Beyond the horizon, an enormous blue planet was rising, tilted at an angle and surrounded by glistening rings that reached high into the sky.

"The thirteenth planet," Mazzy breathed.

"So I suppose this must be a moon?" Thomas ventured. He had crept to the edge and was peering down at a huge temple complex far below, ruined now and overgrown.

"The home of the Drax," said Mazzy. "Or it was, once. Now it's just— *Whoa!*"

She stumbled back from the doorway as an enormous flying battleship slid across their field of vision, blocking their view. It was a grimy wall of cannons and oily pistons pumping up and down, and it seethed black smoke from its vents.

"That's a *Mechanic battleship!*" Mazzy almost screamed.

They stared in terror as the massive war machine loomed alongside the tiny gunship. The stink of it wafted over them, the stench of burning grease and toxic fumes. It was carrying enough firepower to destroy them a hundred times over. Any moment now they expected it to open fire and blast them out of the sky.

But it didn't. Ranks of guns passed them by, but none of them fired. The battleship hung there in the air but did nothing.

"Why haven't we been blown up yet?" Thomas asked quietly.

"I don't think they've seen us," Jack said.

"But, um, we're right here," Thomas replied, puzzled.

Mazzy was wearing an amazed expression. "We're cloaked. We're invisible."

"Like how the Epsilon was invisible when you were in the forest!" Thomas said.

"Yes, but that was when we were still. You can cloak an aircraft when it's not moving. But to cloak one that's flying through the air . . ." She whistled. "He did say it was built for stealth. Whoever the Hexagram are, they've got some serious tech."

They flew onward, keeping a steady pace. Behind the first battleship was a second, bristling with weapons. They were guards, ready to destroy anyone who came through the rift gate without permission. Gradius's gunship flew right past them, unnoticed.

Jack watched them dwindle into the distance. So the Mechanics were here, on the thirteenth planet. He remembered the sketches he had made back on Earth, terrifying creatures that were half metal and half flesh, and wondered what he had gotten himself into.

· ◦ ✦ ◦ ·

The land became poisoned and foul as they flew toward their destination, and the forests withered and died and finally disappeared altogether. By the time they set down, in a hollow near the edge of a plunging cliff, the air smelled like rotten eggs and the horizon was blurred by a yellowish haze. Gradius clambered out of the cockpit and met them as they emerged. He was wearing a sword in a sheath on his back, and he carried a pair of blasters in holsters.

"We go on foot from here," he said.

"Where are we going?" Thomas asked.

Gradius walked to the edge of the cliff and pointed down. "There," he said.

They joined him and saw below them a blasted landscape scarred by half a dozen open-cast mines, great holes in the earth with stepped sides. Diggers scraped at the rock, and six-wheeled trucks rumbled up the ramps between the levels. In the midst of the mines was a facility of some kind, a mass of chimneys and pipes and spiked fences, surrounded by junkyards. Vats of acid bubbled and steamed, furnaces glowed with heat, and rattling conveyor belts carried bits and pieces from building to building. A dirty haze hung close to the ground, and it was hard to see the workers who moved in the yards, but Jack could see enough to tell that they walked jerkily and seemed strangely misshapen. He didn't want to see them any closer.

"The gunship's sensors picked this place up as soon as we arrived," said Gradius. "Hard to hide that much pollution."

"What are they doing here?" Jack asked, aghast.

Mazzy's face had gone grim. "What they always do," she said. "What they did to my home planet. They kill the soil, they foul up the air, they strip every last thing they can use . . . and they build more machines."

"This is what they'll do to the whole of the Nexus, unless we can stop them," said Gradius.

"Wait a minute," said Thomas. "Isn't *Earth* in the Nexus?"

"Barely," said Mazzy. "But, yeah, they'll get you, too, in the end."

"Let's get down there, then," said Jack grimly. "Nobody messes with Earth."

They made their way down from the cliffs and approached the facility via a dried-up riverbed that zigzagged along the cracked and lifeless plain. Drifting clouds of exhaust smoke and piles of junk made it easy to remain unobserved. They spotted things prowling in the distance between the junk heaps, tall, four-legged creatures with huge jaws and lumbering, oddly shaped giants, but they were only dim shapes in the murk.

The facility was surrounded by a tall fence of solid metal, bristling with rusty spikes. They followed it around till they came to a small side gate, but the gate was shut and locked.

"There's a keypad," said Gradius. "It needs a passcode."

"Well, how do we get in?"

Gradius was digging in the pockets of his pants. "I should be able to use my decoder . . ."

Mazzy snorted and pushed past him. She pulled out the data cable from her wrist and plugged it into the side of the box. The numbers blinked frantically, and then the gate clicked open. "I *am* a decoder," she said.

Gradius stared at her in admiration. "I'm glad you came, after all," he said.

"Just get me to a terminal," she said. "If there's anything about Firehawk in their system, I'll find it."

There were guards inside, but Gradius was a pro at dodging guards. Somehow he always seemed to know when they were coming around the corner and took the group another way or found them a niche to hide in till the danger had passed.

"I've had a lot of practice," he said, by way of explanation.

Jack was glad of it. It was the first time he had seen Mechanics up close, and they made him sick with fear. They were horrible ogres of grimy iron and pasty white flesh, like something out of a nightmare. There was just enough left of them to be recognizable as human; the rest was pipes and pumps and gears, whirring mechanical eyes and metal claws and metal jaws.

"Is that what'll happen to us if they catch us?" Thomas whimpered.

"If you're lucky," said Mazzy.

They went deeper into the facility, surrounded by the sounds of clanking and grinding and gasps of steam. Jack stuck close to Thomas, who seemed like he was ready to bolt at any moment. When Thomas looked to him for reassurance, Jack gave him a confident smile. Being brave for someone else's sake was easier than being brave on your own.

As they were passing a doorway, Gradius, who was leading the way, suddenly froze. "Back! Back!" he hissed, and he hurried them into a hiding place between two huge vertical pipes a moment before the door screeched open and two people emerged.

"I'm leaving you in charge, Vardis. The Colonel wants to see me immediately," said a woman's voice. The two of them stopped in the corridor, just out of sight.

"You can't go now!" Vardis said. The voice was an electronic croak, filtered through a mask.

"The Colonel wants me to be the face of the broadcast they're going to make across the Nexus," she said.

"But the Firehawk is due to launch at dawn."

"Exactly. Which is why I must be on Braxis Prime, ready to broadcast to our enemies, to show them the unstoppable power of our new weapon. No doubt you can handle things without me. It's all automated, anyway."

"General Kara, I think this is a mistake," said Vardis. Jack, who was squeezed up close to Mazzy, felt her go rigid at the mention of that name. Her jaw went tight with rage.

"Tell that to the Colonel," said Kara. "Don't worry. Nothing will go wrong. By the time they see it coming, it will be too late."

Jack threw his arms around Mazzy as she tried to lunge out from their hiding place. Gradius, seeing the danger, clamped a hand over her mouth. Together they held her as she fought against them. Only the pounding din of the facility prevented their struggle from being heard.

"I'll see you afterward, Vardis," said Kara, and she walked off down the corridor. Vardis went the other way. Through a gap in the pipes, Jack caught a brief glimpse of him as he passed, dressed all in black, his face a mirrored mask. For an instant, Jack saw his own face reflected there. But Vardis passed by without seeing them, turned a corner, and was gone. Only then did they let Mazzy go.

"That was her!" Mazzy snapped. "The woman who betrayed my planet! That might have been my only chance!"

"To do what?" Jack said. "Get us all killed?"

"She cost me my parents!" Mazzy raged. "I can't let her get away with that!"

"Then we'll get her, okay? We'll get her somehow. But not now."

"You heard her," said Gradius. "The Firehawk launches at dawn. And it's some kind of weapon. We have to stop them."

Mazzy swore under her breath. "All right," she said through gritted teeth. "Kara can wait."

Jack warily released her. "Why don't we see what they were doing in that room, huh?"

They slipped out from their hiding place and opened the door that Kara and Vardis had emerged from. Inside was a room with several large screens. Lined up in seats along the edges, working at consoles, were a dozen spindly robots that looked like they had been assembled from broken-down tractors and bits you might find in the back of the garage. They jerked back and forth in their seats, tiny heads bobbing awkwardly on their necks as their fingers stabbed stiffly at the controls.

"Jackpot," said Gradius. "There must be something here you can plug into, Mazzy?"

"Er, what about them?" asked Thomas, eyeing the robots.

"Drones," said Mazzy distastefully as she walked into the room. "Don't worry. They're too stupid to recognize us." She found an unoccupied screen and plugged in the data cable from her wrist. Information began scrolling across her eyes. "I'll just be a minute."

Jack watched the drones nervously, tapping his feet. At any moment he expected them to lurch to their feet and attack, but they just ignored him. Thomas looked restless. Jack could tell he wanted to go and fiddle with something.

"Don't," he warned.

Thomas huffed. Eager for distraction, he turned his attention to Gradius. "Hey," he said. "So who's the Colonel? Is he like the leader of the Mechanics?"

"The Kernel. And yes."

"The Colonel, that's what I said."

"Kernel. With a *K*. Like in a nut. It means the central and most important part of something."

"How could you tell I was spelling it wrong? They're pronounced exactly the same."

"I just knew."

"Oh. All right, then: the Kernel. Who's he?"

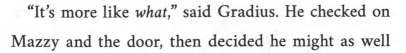

"It's more like *what*," said Gradius. He checked on Mazzy and the door, then decided he might as well tell the story. "Braxis Prime wasn't always the home of the Mechanics. The Braxians were a race of engineers and mathematicians who were responsible for some of the greatest inventions in the Nexus. It was even rumored that they knew how to create antimatter, the most potent and dangerous source of energy ever known. Just a few pounds of that stuff could power a whole city for a hundred years, they said." His face hardened. "Trouble is, they got a bit too fond of their own inventions. They decided that people weren't much good at dealing with their own problems, so they built a giant artificial intelligence to run their planet for them. They called it the Kernel."

He produced a small scroll of thin, transparent material and pulled it out. It hardened immediately into an almost invisible screen. He tapped a few icons and then showed them a picture of a green-and-brown planet, a lot like Earth, except the continents were different shapes.

"Braxis Prime, around the time the Kernel went online."

He tapped a button. Now large portions of the land had turned brown, and there were black clouds hanging over them.

"This is two months after, just before they shut the rift gate and stopped anyone getting through to help."

He tapped again. Now all the lands were covered in brown. The seas had shrunk, and the planet was shrouded in murk. "This was taken from the last of the Braxian spy satellites before it went offline. As far as we know, the seas have gone now, too. The Braxians . . . well, you saw the guards. No doubt the planet's population were all converted into something more . . . useful."

"What is that brown stuff?" Jack asked, appalled.

"Machinery," he said. "Machinery and junk. The whole planet is covered in it."

"And the Kernel is somewhere on that planet?"

Gradius gave him a humorless smile. "You don't get it. All that machinery, it's like a giant network, tunneling into the earth, spreading over the whole of the world. The Kernel isn't *on* the planet. It *is* the planet."

"Got something!" Mazzy said, pulling the cable out. It whizzed back into her wrist as she walked over to

225

them. Jack could tell she was still angry about missing the chance to get to General Kara.

"You found the Firehawk?" Gradius asked.

"Maybe. There's nothing on it in the system—it must be ultra-secret—but there's a lot of traffic and deliveries going from this facility to a location just a little way from here. I tracked their GPS signals. I don't know what's there, but I wouldn't be surprised if it's what we're looking for."

"Good work!" said Gradius, giving her a brilliant smile. Jack wondered if he was capable of smiling like that. "Let's go, then!"

"Not yet. We have something to do here first."

"More important than saving the Nexus from whatever devastating weapon the Mechanics have cooked up?" Gradius asked testily.

"Yep," said Mazzy. "Looks like the Hunters caught the Epsilon, after all. Boston, Dunk, and Ilara are right here, in the cells down below. And we're going to get them out."

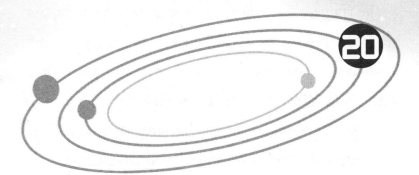

Mazzy had plotted them a route through the facility down to the cells, taking them by lesser-used ways to avoid the guards. Locked doors had been opened to let them past, others jammed shut to prevent anyone from wandering into their path. Cameras watched them with glassy eyes, but they saw nothing: Mazzy had deactivated them all.

"They must have captured them and brought them here," said Mazzy. "I guess Scorch and the Changeling are in on the Mechanics' plan, too."

"So the Hunters are here?" Thomas asked, sounding worried.

"Probably."

The Hunters who killed my parents, Jack thought, and he wondered at how easily he'd slipped back into thinking of them as such, now that there was no alternative left. What did it matter what they were made of, in the end? Plenty of people with flesh-and-blood parents had a much worse time of it than he had.

The news fired him up. He was eager to prove himself. All he had left of his life was the Earth he'd grown up on and the memory of his parents. He'd fight for both of them. You had to fight for something.

"What happened to the Epsilon?" Jack asked.

"It's locked down in a dock nearby." She tapped her head. "But I have the release code now."

"Why didn't they just blow them out of the sky?" Gradius wondered.

"Maybe they spared them because they thought they knew where the famous Gradius Clench might be found," said Jack sourly. "After all, that's why we're all being hunted."

Gradius flashed him a grin. "Well, in that case I saved their lives, didn't I?"

Jack glared at his back as Gradius strode off ahead, humming to himself. Thomas tentatively offered his inhaler. Jack waved it away.

Dad would have loved you, he thought bitterly at Gradius.

Mazzy led them onward, her face grim with determination. They took a clanking elevator to the lower levels, where the darkness was barely relieved by flickering yellow lights in cages, and vents oozed a foul-smelling steam that made Thomas complain about his sinuses. Some of the doorways were blocked with dirty iron portcullises, which screeched open with startling speed when they pressed the touchpads nearby.

"The cells are close," Mazzy said as she led them through a wide chamber where thick black pipes ran along the roof, dripping moisture. "Careful, though. They've got Gristlers loose down here."

"Gristlers?" Thomas asked nervously.

"Monsters created by the Mechanics, half flesh and

bone and half machine, bred for mindless savagery," Gradius said.

"Is that one?" asked Thomas, pointing. They followed his finger to a doorway, where a hunched creature like a massive hyena had just loped into the room. Its legs and the ridge of its spine were metal, there were exposed cables at its neck, and its brassy eyes whirred and glowed green in the dark. Quivering lips peeled back over dripping fangs as it saw them.

"Yep," said Mazzy. "Run?"

Gradius grabbed Thomas's collar before he could take her advice. "Run and it'll chase you," he said. "You won't win that race."

"I'm willing to try!" Thomas wheezed, straining at his collar like a stubborn puppy.

"Back off," Gradius told them, his gaze fixed on the Gristler. "All of you, slowly. Back the way we came."

Jack hated the coolness and authority in that voice. He didn't want to do as he was told. To obey would be like admitting Gradius was in charge. But the sight of the Gristler drove any better ideas out of his head. He had no idea how to fight that thing, so in the end, he shuffled toward the exit with Mazzy and Thomas. Gradius detached himself from the group and walked carefully the other way, out into the center of the chamber.

The Gristler growled at Jack and took a menacing step toward him.

"Hey! Over here!" said Gradius, waving his hands. "It's me you want!"

The beast's attention wavered between Gradius and the others. It seemed to be deciding which was the better target. Then Gradius clapped his hands and whistled at it, and that made up its mind. With a growl, it broke into a charge, heading for Gradius.

"Go!" he shouted at the others, and they ran through the doorway as the creature bore down on him. Mazzy slapped her hand on the touchpad on the other side, and the portcullis rattled down behind them, cutting them off from the chamber, leaving Gradius alone with the beast.

Jack clutched the bars and watched, aghast, as the monster opened its jaws to snatch up Gradius. But the jaws snapped shut on nothing; Gradius had rolled aside, moving so fast that Jack had to blink to be sure he'd seen it. The creature swerved with a howl and snapped at him again, but Gradius backflipped and landed smoothly on his feet.

"He's like a ninja!" Thomas gasped.

"He's all right," Jack said grudgingly. "I mean, he wouldn't win at the Olympics or anything."

"Don't you have blasters and a sword?" Mazzy called to Gradius.

Gradius backward-rolled to avoid a lashing tail and surged back to his feet again. He gave her a wink. "I've got another way."

With that, he sprinted toward the doorway that the Gristler had come through. The beast roared and gave chase, thumping after him on metal paws.

"Run like hell? That's his plan?" Jack muttered. "Wow."

Mazzy whacked him on the arm. "Can you give him some support? He's trying to save our lives here!"

"I bet *I* could save our lives if you gave me a chance," Jack grumbled under his breath. But he knew it was a lie. The more he watched Gradius, the more certain he became that he would never be the boy his parents had wanted him to be, that he couldn't ever live up to their expectations.

Gradius was fast, but the beast was faster. In a few bounds it closed the distance between them. It leaped for Gradius just as he reached the doorway, but he threw himself into a slide and skidded through on his hip, slapping the touchpad as he went by. The portcullis thundered down just as the Gristler passed beneath it, catching it in midair and slamming it to the ground. The creature was pinned to the floor by the portcullis spikes, twitching feebly, its jaws opening and closing inches from Gradius's legs. Then it gave a long wheeze, and the light in its eyes went out.

"Whoa," said Thomas, amazed.

Mazzy palmed the touchpad and let them back into the chamber. "I have to admit, that was seriously impressive," she said.

Gradius was back on his feet and dusting himself off. "All in a day's work," he said modestly. He tried the touchpad again, but the portcullis only made a grinding noise and didn't move. It was jammed by the body of the Gristler. "Guess I'm stuck on this side. I'll make my own way around, meet you at the cells." He gave them a quick salute and disappeared.

"See you there," said Mazzy. She looked back at Jack and raised an eyebrow expectantly.

"What?" Jack said, shrugging. "All he did was single-handedly kill a seven-hundred-pound death machine. It wasn't that great."

· · ✦ · ·

"Mazzy!" Boston cried as the door to his cell slid open and he saw her standing there.

"Rescued by a bunch of kids," said Mazzy, shaking her head in mock despair. "This is a new low, Boston."

He grinned at her, rushed over, and swept her up in a hug. Jack was pleased to see her hug him back with genuine affection. The closeness between the ragtag crew of the Epsilon gave him hope for the future. He'd never experienced anything like that before, and he wanted to be near it. He wanted to be *part* of it.

"I can't believe you found us!" Boston said.

"What, you thought I'd leave you behind?"

"We did leave them behind, actually," Thomas pointed out. "When we decided to go with Gradius to—"

Jack put a hand over his mouth.

"Gradius Clench is here?" Boston asked.

"Are you kidding?" Jack cried. "We turn up to save you from certain death and all you can do is ask about Gradius Clench?"

"Don't mind him; he's jealous," Mazzy told Boston.

"I am *not* jealous!"

"Envious, then."

"I need to make sure the others are okay." Boston led them to the next cell. Like the first, it was nothing more than a solid metal door with a number stenciled on it.

"The Epsilon still had a damaged thruster from when we escaped them on Earth. We couldn't outrun them, even in Combat Mode, so we had to surrender," Boston told the group. "I thought they were going to kill us. Turns out TOF-1 reported that he was chasing you through the temple, but they lost contact after that."

"Yeah, he got eaten," said Jack, with some satisfaction.

"I know. Scorch and the Changeling found his blunderbuss at the temple in the end. There was no sign of you, but they saw the star map and figured you'd had some help escaping. They took us here for questioning to find out what we knew, maybe see if we could get them any closer to Gradius Clench."

Mazzy plugged her cable into the keypad, and the lock beeped. They pulled it open. Dunk was standing just inside the door, glaring, as if he'd been expecting them the whole time.

"I'd better be getting compensation for this," he told them. "Being kidnapped counts as overtime, you know. Union rules."

"Hello to you, too," said Mazzy. "Where's Ilara?"

"They took her to a special shielded cell, down the way," said Boston, pointing. "Something that dampens her Host powers. They didn't want her mind-controlling the guards."

"Well, let's go fetch her. It's only a matter of time before the Mechanics catch on to us."

They hurried down the corridor until they came to a cell door that was painted with yellow-and-black stripes, with the words *extreme hazard* printed across them.

"Sounds like Ilara," said Boston. "Mazzy, would you?"

Mazzy saw to the lock and they opened the door. Inside, Ilara sat rigidly in a large metal seat that hummed with power. Her hood had been thrown back, and a band of metal surrounded her head. She stared blankly ahead and did not seem to see them.

"Get her out of there," Boston snarled, hurrying inside. Mazzy went with him. In moments they had found a switch and deactivated the chair. As soon as the band around her forehead had been removed, Ilara slumped forward.

"Aaaa! There's a giant slug on her head!" Thomas squealed as he saw the bloated, brightly striped creature attached to the back of Ilara's bald skull, reaching from the crown of her head to the nape of her neck. "Get it off!"

"Oh, that?" said Dunk. "That's supposed to be there."

"It is?"

Dunk scratched a spot on his nose. "The Hosts let those slug things attach to their babies when they're young. They grow up together. It's what gives 'em the powers to read minds and whatnot. Disgusting, if you ask me."

"Ilara, are you all right?" Mazzy asked as they lifted her out of her chair. "What did they do to you?"

Ilara's eyes focused and she looked around wildly as she recovered. "Are . . . are they gone? Are you really here?" Then she broke into a smile of relieved gratitude. "Thank you! Thank you for saving me! I don't know what would have happened if you hadn't come!"

Boston and Mazzy exchanged an uncertain glance. "Erm . . . you're welcome," said Boston.

"They must really have shaken you up, huh?" Mazzy said.

Jack caught the strange look between Boston and Mazzy and wondered at its meaning, but he soon forgot about it. Now that the crew was all together again, and everyone was safe, they grinned in relief and slapped one another on the back. Boston shook Jack's hand and Thomas's, too, and even Dunk grudgingly thanked them.

Jack beamed like an idiot. It felt so good to be included in that warmth. No longer were he and Thomas a pair of useless hostages; they'd proved their worth now. He began to wonder if maybe he *could* be part of this, after all.

"Ah, good!" said Gradius, who had appeared in the doorway. "Looks like we're all here, then. We might want to get going. The elevator's on its way down, and I'm betting there'll be a whole heap of guards here soon."

Boston did a double take from Gradius to Jack and back again. "He *does* look like you," he told Jack. He checked them both again. "Better haircut, though. Nicer teeth, too."

"So happy you noticed," said Gradius, giving him a dazzling smile. "Now, shall we?" He invited them out of the cell.

"Right! Back to the Epsilon, and let's get out of here!" Boston said.

"Not quite," said Gradius. "Mazzy? I believe you owe me the location of a certain Firehawk? They are launching at dawn, remember?"

"Oh yeah," said Mazzy, giving Boston a sheepish look. "Sorry. Escape will have to wait. We have to save the universe first."

Boston rolled his eyes. "It's always *something*, isn't it?"

21

It was not far to the mysterious location Mazzy had discovered in the facility's computer records, but they were forced to go on foot. There were too many of them for Gradius's tiny gunship to carry, especially since Dunk weighed as much as the rest of them put together. They slipped away under cover of the drifting smoke, with the wail of alarms rising behind them.

To stay unobserved they were forced to take a route up a sharp ridge and back into the rocky peaks, where narrow paths ran alongside jagged gullies. Toxic sludge bubbled and blorped at the bottom, belching wafts of eggy stench up at them as they passed. It was hard going, but necessary, because the Mechanics were looking for them now. Several times they were forced to hide from surveillance robots cruising menacingly overhead.

"You're muttering," Thomas told Jack.

"I am not muttering," he muttered, glaring at Gradius's back.

"You are so. You've been muttering to yourself for five minutes now."

Jack kicked at a stone and said nothing. The poison in the air made his eyes sting.

"Why don't you like him?" Thomas asked.

"Who?"

"Gradius, dummy. It's obvious."

Jack shrugged.

"I mean, he's pretty cool, right?" said Thomas. "And he's a good guy to have on our side. It must be like finding a long-lost brother for you, right? I wish *I* had a brother."

"He's *not* like a brother. Didn't you hear him? We're clones!"

"Well, a twin, then! That's even better!"

"No, it's not!" Jack said, exasperated. He struggled to think how to explain it. "Look, we started off exactly the same, right? Identical in every way. Except *he* turned out to be some superbad awesome hero of the galaxy with, like, perfect hair and a warehouse full of confidence, and I turned out to be . . . *me*. Just some kid who can draw a little. Don't you get it? He's like a living monument to what I could have been, if only I'd tried harder, done better. He's like a better version of me, and that makes me . . . that makes me the worse version. The reject. The *spare*."

"Now, that's not entirely fair," said Thomas. "Sure, you might have started off the same, but you grew up on two different planets. Who knows how different his life was from yours? He was probably getting massaged by weird octopus women after his workout while you were getting elbow dropped by some doofus in a tracksuit."

"That's my dad!" Jack thought for a moment. "Was."

"Sorry. Look, I'm just saying, you can't compare yourself to someone you don't really know. Everyone can make themselves look like things are going great if they put in a little effort. Besides, it wasn't *him* who saved me from the Fangbeast. Remember that? I'd have been eaten for sure if it wasn't for you. You risked your own life to save me. That was the coolest thing I ever saw." He poked Jack in the chest. "I don't care if he's a superbad awesome hero of the galaxy. I'd rather have you as my friend any day."

Jack couldn't keep down a smile at that. "Huh. I suppose that was pretty cool, wasn't it?"

"Sure was. So why don't you stop acting like there's only space for one of you? You can *both* be superbad awesome heroes if you want to."

"Thanks, Thomas," said Jack, feeling better. "Hey, you know, you should be having an asthma attack about now."

"Huh?"

"I mean, all this smoke in the air. And your nose isn't running anymore, either."

Thomas dabbed at his nose in surprise. "But it's *always* running. I mean, so much that if I forget to drink a glass of water at night I dehydrate."

243

"It's not running now. Welcome to the world of dry upper lips."

"What do you think it means?" Thomas asked, amazed.

"You heard what Boston said. We Earthers have amazing immune systems from fighting off all those deadly viruses. Maybe yours couldn't cope with things at home, but with the wussy germs they've got out here, you might never get sick again!"

Thomas's eyes shone. "No more sick days! Think of it! That's like another third of my life I'll get back."

"Maybe we belong out here, you and me," said Jack.

"Yeah," said Thomas. His gaze became distant, and a silly grin spread across his face. "Yeah."

They caught up with Boston, Mazzy, and Ilara, who were a little way ahead of them. Dunk was at the back, complaining to himself, and Gradius kept himself separate from the main group, as if eager to be on his own. Jack remembered how reluctant he had been to bring them along. With the exception of Mazzy, they were deadweight as far as he was concerned.

"You think the Firehawk is really nearby?" Thomas asked Mazzy.

"I know it is," said Ilara, before Mazzy could reply. "I have seen it in our enemy's mind."

"I thought you couldn't use your powers inside that chair?" said Boston.

"They tried to stop me." She smiled. "They didn't try hard enough. I couldn't get much, but I got something. It was General Kara herself who questioned me. I saw in her mind the image of a burning bird, a thing of terrible power, and also . . . a cave."

"A cave?"

"A secret way. The Firehawk is heavily guarded, but there is a route beneath the security fences. An old tunnel. Kara had it in mind as an escape route, if ever she should need one. We can use it to get in unseen."

"Do you know where it is?" Mazzy asked excitedly.

"I believe I do," she said. "Follow me."

They let Ilara take the lead, and she took them by difficult paths down among the peaks. Twice more they had to hide as scout robots passed by overhead, silhouetted against the glowing rings of Braxis Prime.

"It's getting dark," said Jack.

"Oh, those robots can still see us in the dark," said Gradius. "It's just that *we* won't see *them*."

"Speak for yourself," said Mazzy, tapping the side of her eye socket. "Night vision comes as standard on these babies."

The last light of the day was draining from the sky when they came in sight of the Firehawk. They stood on a cliff overlooking a canyon full of poison sludge and stared at it through a crack in the peaks. It was bigger than a battleship, with a colossal wingspan: a vast metal bird resting on a launch ramp, pointed diagonally upward to the sky. Massive thrusters hung beneath its wings and tail.

"The Firehawk is an *aircraft?*" Jack said.

"Huh," said Dunk. "I used to work on building those, back in the factories on Thuvia, before they fired me for crimes against hygiene. It's a cargo hauler. Flies like a drunk whale."

"What good does an aircraft do the Mechanics?" Boston wondered. "The moment it pokes its nose through a rift gate, it'll get blasted to pieces, no matter how big it is."

Mazzy's eyes briefly danced with calculations. "Looks like that's what they mean to do with it, though. It's pointed directly at the rift gate we came through."

"There must be more to it," said Gradius. "We need to get closer. They said they were launching at dawn. That gives us mere hours."

"The cave is down there," said Ilara, pointing. And indeed there was an entrance in the rock, along a path that ran down off the cliff. "Come. We must hurry."

But Boston didn't move. He was studying the cave thoughtfully. "Hey, Ilara," he said. "You remember that time when you and I were in the Silver Mountains on Kadis IV, and we found a cave just like this that turned out to be full of spikebats?"

Ilara gave him a puzzled look. "Yes, I remember," she said. "But I doubt there are any spikebats here."

"I guess not," Boston said, and shoved her off the cliff.

"*Ilaraaaa!*" Mazzy screamed. Ilara screamed, too, flailing at the air as she plummeted into the gully and was swallowed up by the poisonous sludge at the bottom.

"What did you *do*?" Mazzy yelled at Boston. Dunk lumbered over and seized his arms, pulling them up behind his back with an iron grip.

"Oh, hey, easy now!" said Boston, chuckling.

"*Easy now*?" Mazzy cried. "We ought to throw you off that cliff after her!"

Jack stared at Boston in appalled shock. "You killed her!" he said. "You killed Ilara!"

"Relax," said Boston. "Take a look."

They went to the edge of the cliff and looked over. Ilara had broken the surface of the sludge and was waving her arms helplessly. Except it wasn't Ilara anymore. Those elegant features had started to run like wax. Her fingers had melted together into an oozing mush. As Jack watched in horror, Ilara turned into a throbbing blob of shiny slime, long tentacles thrashing wildly in the air as she sank. At last the sludge closed over her head, and there was a loud, stinking burp from below that sent them all reeling back from the edge with their eyes watering.

"Phew!" said Thomas. "So long, Jodie Ellis."

"That was your girlfriend?" Mazzy asked Jack. "The slime creature?"

"She was *not* my girlfriend!" Jack cried.

"It was the Changeling," said Boston. He looked over his shoulder at Dunk. "You feel like letting me go now? I hear medical bills come straight out of your pay packet if you injure your employer."

Dunk let him go as if he were on fire. Boston massaged his shoulders and stepped away, wincing.

"I got suspicious when we saw her in her cell. She's far too high-and-mighty to ever say thank you to someone like me, even if we did just save her life. And that story about Kara didn't ring true, either. Hard to believe the Traitor of Rakkan would be so sloppy as to let a Host read her mind. And why would she need an escape route through a *cave*?"

"But what if you'd been wrong? How could you be sure?" Mazzy asked.

"We never went to the Silver Mountains on Kadis IV," said Boston. "And spikebats? I just made them up."

"So the whole thing was a setup?" Jack asked.

"They figured you'd come for us and left the Changeling there to lead us into a trap. I expect that inside that cave we'd find a *lot* of Mechanics waiting for us. So I think we'll take another route, huh?"

"Smart work," said Gradius. "Well done."

"Thanks, kid," said Boston, ruffling his hair. Jack would have given a lot to be able to get a photo of the look on Gradius's face right then.

"So if it wasn't Ilara," said Dunk, "where's Ilara?"

Boston pointed toward the Firehawk. "In there, probably. Shall we go find out?"

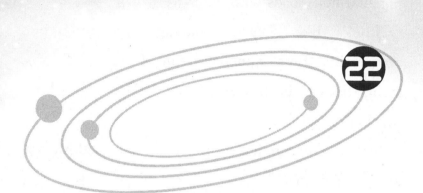

22

The cargo bay of the Firehawk was a smoky cavern, echoing with engines. Robot vehicles rolled back and forth down the ramp while Mechanic laborers loaded them up using their powerful hydraulic arms. In the frenzy of activity, nobody noticed a handful of stowaways sneaking away from one of the vehicles, to hide behind a pile of junk in a corner.

"What are they doing?" Thomas wondered, peering in horror at the Mechanics. They were a mix of meat and machinery, things who had once been human but whose bodies and faces had mostly been replaced with parts that looked like they came from rusty digger trucks. They snarled and glared as they worked, lifting enormous loads with ease.

"Looks like they're clearing everything out before this thing launches," said Gradius. "Everything that can be salvaged, they'll take. That's how Mechanics are."

"But they're bringing things in as well," said Mazzy. She pointed. "See?"

As they watched, several Mechanics unloaded an enormous metal cylinder from the back of a particularly large vehicle. There were thick, riveted windows in the side, like portholes, and within they could see a strange sparkling substance that hurt the eyes to look at. It was like the afterimage of the sun, or the negative of a photograph: burning bright, but all the colors seemed somehow reversed.

"Is that . . ." Boston gasped.

"Antimatter," said Gradius grimly.

"The rumors were true, then? The Braxians knew how to make antimatter? The most powerful energy source in the universe?"

"I guess they did," said Gradius. "And since they all got turned into Mechanics, that means the Mechanics know, too." He got to his feet. "Let's follow that cylinder. I want to know what they're doing with it."

They made their way around the edge of the room, moving between stacks of junk to avoid the gaze of the Mechanics. Mazzy spotted a service hatch high up on one wall that looked like it might lead into the next chamber, where the cylinder of antimatter had gone. One by one, they clambered up the ladder and slipped inside, concealed by the fog of engine fumes that hung in the air.

"Y'know, if the Mechanics weren't so dirty, they'd be a lot harder to sneak past," Jack mused, stifling a cough with his fist.

The service hatch led to a walkway that crossed another huge chamber, high up in the air. When it was Jack's turn to climb, he found Gradius and Boston crouched on it, looking gravely down. Their faces were lit from below with an eerie white light. In the chamber, stacked in haphazard piles, were hundreds of cylinders, just like the one they had seen earlier.

The whole room seethed with the strange glow of antimatter.

"This is bad," said Boston.

"You can say that again," said Gradius.

"I think I pretty much summed it up the first time, actually."

Jack slid up close to them and looked over the edge of the walkway. Mechanics moved about between the piles. Scattered among the cylinders were several larger devices, huge metal tanks covered in cables and lights.

"What are those?" he asked, pointing.

"I think they're bombs," said Gradius. "I think this aircraft is just one giant bomb."

Jack went pale. "You said that a few pounds of that stuff could power a city for a hundred years," he said. "What could that much antimatter do?"

"There's enough here to blow up a planet," said Boston. "This much antimatter, all released at once . . . it would be like a supernova. If they flew this through a rift gate, it wouldn't *matter* if it got blown to bits within seconds, because it would take the *whole planet* with it."

Gradius's eyes were flinty. "We have to stop this," he said.

"Well, duh," said Jack.

. . ✛ . .

There was no way to get near the piles of anti-matter without being seen by the Mechanics, and there were too many bombs to disable before dawn even if they could. They had to seek another way to prevent the disaster to come. They headed into the depths of the Firehawk, where the corridors became emptier. Most of the Mechanics were in the cargo bay preparing to leave, it seemed. Only a few were left patrolling the quiet, cold passageways farther in.

"If we can't stop the bombs, what can we do?" Thomas asked.

"We can stop the Firehawk from taking off. That might buy us some time, at least," said Gradius.

"And we have to find Ilara, too," said Jack. "She's nearby, I'm sure of it."

Gradius gave him a funny look. "What makes you so certain?"

Jack frowned. "I don't know. I just know. She's over near the scanner bay."

"That's a total guess!"

"It is, isn't it?" said Jack. He was as puzzled as anyone. "But I'm sure. I mean it. I'm dead sure."

"We don't have time to go running off to investigate a hunch," Gradius said impatiently. "This w—"

"Scanner bay, you said?" Dunk talked over him, addressing Jack. "Lead on."

"Didn't you hear me? We have to get to engineering, sabotage the engines!"

"Sorry, fella," said Dunk. "We're going to find Ilara. And the day I listen to management over a working joe, like Jack here, is the day I hand in my union card."

"I'm going, too!" said Thomas. "I love hunches!"

"And me," said Mazzy. "Ilara's a friend. Or, like, a crewmate, at least. Maybe just an acquaintance, actually." She frowned. "In fact, she's kind of a pain, but we're going to get her, anyway."

"But I might need you to disable the locks in engineering!" Gradius protested.

"Tough," said Mazzy, heading off after the others.

Boston shrugged at Gradius as he followed. "The people have spoken."

"Amateurs!" Gradius cried in exasperation, but in the end he had no choice but to go with them.

Jack could hardly keep the smile off his face. *You might be the big-shot hero, Gradius,* he thought, *but the rest of us, we're a team.*

He made his way through the corridors as if he'd known them all his life. It was a strange feeling. He was being *drawn,* pulled along by a relentless curiosity to see what was behind a certain door in the scanner bay. By the time they reached it, he was practically jigging with anticipation.

"You think she's in there?" Mazzy asked.

"I have no reason to think so," said Jack. "But she definitely is."

"Good enough for me," said Mazzy. She put her cable into the keypad and the door unlocked.

Inside, Ilara sat rigidly in a large metal seat that hummed with power. Her hood had been thrown back and a band of metal surrounded her head. She stared blankly ahead and did not seem to see them.

"*The Changeling!*" Thomas screamed. He pulled Boston's blaster out from its holster and pointed it at Ilara's face. Mazzy snatched it off him before he could work out how to fire it and handed it irritably back to Boston.

"Let's just see before we shoot her, eh?" said Jack, patting him on the shoulder. Thomas took a few calming sucks on his empty inhaler while the others disconnected her from the chair and helped her stand.

"It's about time you all got here," said Ilara, annoyed. "What were you doing, playing cards or something?"

"*That's* our Ilara!" said Boston. Impulsively he reached to hug her, but the withering stare she gave him made him reconsider. "Yep, definitely her."

"Of course I'm Ilara, you fool. What are you talking about?"

"Long story," said Boston.

"All right, I'll just read your mind, then."

"Wait, no, don't!" Boston cried, but it was too late. Ilara's face turned to a picture of horror.

"It's been *how* many days since you washed your underwear?" she asked in disgust.

"I ran out of briefs!" Boston cried. "I've been busy!"

Ilara turned away, dismissing him with a shake of the head. "Humans!" she sniffed. "Do you know how hard it was to reach out to your minds and lead you to me with that machine trying to block me?" She looked at Jack, and Jack was surprised to see the barest hint of a smile there. "At least *someone* was listening," she said.

Jack smiled back at her. All of a sudden, she didn't seem quite so scary.

There was a crackle of static and a blare of horns from out in the corridor. The kind of music that usually meant an official announcement was about to be made.

"What's that?" asked Thomas, already hurrying out to investigate. Jack followed him, in case he fiddled with anything that shouldn't be fiddled with, and the rest came after.

They traced the noise to a video screen in a small control room for monitoring the scanners. As they arrived, the introduction was just ending, and the screen switched to show General Kara standing in front of a grim landscape of factories beneath a filthy brown sky.

"Is that . . . Braxis Prime? The home of the Mechanics?" Thomas said.

"Wouldn't like to be a travel agent for that place," said Jack. "And they said Earth was bad."

"Cholera. Syphilis. Spanish flu. Rabies. Ebola." Dunk was ticking fatal diseases off his fingers.

"Oh, shut up."

"*Everyone* shut up," Gradius told them. "I want to hear what she says."

Mazzy's eyes darkened with hatred as Kara began to speak, her half-human face staring into the camera.

"Citizens of the Nexus," she said. "For too long you have refused the call to become part of the machine. Obsessed with your own selfish lives, you deny the wishes of the Kernel, who would make us all one. One race, one people, together. All of us, using the planets of the Nexus as they were meant to be, as fuel for greater things. Together we would break away from the need to use rift gates. Together we would build giant spacecraft powered by antimatter. Together we would learn to navigate the stars! But you . . . you fear change. And we need the resources of your planets. So we are bringing change to you.

"In less than one hour, we will stage a demonstration of our power. We will destroy one of the planets of the Nexus entirely. There is nothing you can do to stop it. You have only to watch. After that, you will surrender, let the armies of the Mechanics occupy your lands, and submit to the necessary conversion. You will have no choice. The alternative is annihilation. And as you will see, we now have the capability to wipe you out, whenever we choose."

She leaned in close to the camera, and for the first time there was a glimmer of emotion in her eye, a glint of wicked enjoyment.

"Citizens of the Nexus, enjoy the show."

A terrifying boom made them jump, and the corridor began shaking violently all around them. They stumbled this way and that, grabbing on to whatever they could as a deafening roar filled the Firehawk.

"What's going ooooon?" Thomas wailed, clinging to a pillar like a koala made of Scotch tape.

"The Firehawk!" Gradius yelled. "It's launching!"

"That can't be right!" Jack yelled back. "Kara said it wouldn't launch till dawn! It's only been an hour since the sun went down!"

"Oh no," said Mazzy, her face going slack as she realized what was happening. She stumbled over to the video screen, swaying unsteadily as she punched buttons. The picture changed to the view from an outside camera, which was shaking and shuddering. Over the horizon, they saw the edge of a newly rising sun. It was twice as large as when it had gone down.

"How did it get bigger? How is it coming back up?" Thomas howled.

"Remember the star map?" said Mazzy. "Remember we saw the thirteenth planet? It had *two* suns. Night must only last an hour here!"

"So we're stuck in this thing?" Boston cried. "We're stuck on a giant bomb that's headed through the rift gate to blow up a planet?"

"That's about the size of it," said Mazzy. Her eyes began to scroll with numbers. "Calculating chances of survival . . ."

"Don't bother, we already know," said Jack.

"What do we do? What do we do?" Thomas cried.

"We get to the bridge," said Gradius. "Maybe we can't stop this thing from launching, but we can stop it getting to wherever it's going. If we reach the central computer, Mazzy can redirect it. Right?"

Mazzy's eyes cleared. "Right. I hope."

"Then let's go. We should be able to make it as long as the guards haven't noticed we're here yet."

An alarm began to blare in the distance. "Intruders on board! The prisoner is missing! All guards to full alert!"

"Now that," said Dunk, "is bad timing."

Jack ran for his life as a hail of blaster fire streaked over his head. The others were crammed into cover in doorways on either side of the passage. Boston reached out as Jack approached and hauled him roughly in, just before a blaster bolt sizzled through the air where his head had been. He collapsed against the wall, gasping.

"Not that way," he said.

Lumbering after him were six Mechanics. Two of them were enormous, ogre-like laborer types, while the others were smaller and almost entirely made of metal, with only a few patches of pale flesh left to show they were ever anything but robots. They carried energy rifles and cannons, and they weren't shy about using them.

"Here," said Gradius, handing Jack a spare blaster pistol that looked to Jack like a toy gun. Then he leaned out and shot one of the Mechanics square in the chest. The others fled into cover and hid there, taking potshots down the passageway.

"Is there another way around?" Boston called over the rumble and shake of the Firehawk as it powered its way through the sky.

"Only way to the bridge is through this corridor," said Dunk. "The other bulkheads seal up for security when the alarm goes off."

"Can't you control them or make them shoot each other or something?" Jack asked Mazzy. "They're half machine, after all."

"I can hack into anything if I can access it remotely," said Mazzy. "Like TOF-1's monocle. But Mechanics use old-school tech that you have to plug into, precisely to stop people like me from getting into it. I can't even access the plans for this craft without finding a terminal to jack into."

"It's like my phone. You can never get a signal when you need one," Thomas commiserated.

Jack was turning over the blaster in his hand, frantically trying to find the trigger. Gradius grabbed the barrel and steered it away from him. "Careful where you're pointing that."

"How do I even fire this thing?"

"There's a thumb stud on the side. There. Have a go."

Jack found the stud, then, feeling suitably armed, he popped up from behind the pipes and aimed a shot at the Mechanics. A volley of blaster fire sent him cringing back into cover.

Ilara examined her fingernails. "Is this going to take much longer?"

"You could help, you know," said Boston.

"But you're all handling it so well," she purred sarcastically.

Boston exchanged a glance with Mazzy. "See why it was so easy to kick her off a cliff?"

"Yes, and don't think I didn't notice that when I read your mind," she said. "You were *awfully* eager to—"

They flinched as a blaster bolt hit a pipe nearby with a scream of energy. When Jack's shoulders had un-hunched and he opened his eyes again, he saw that there was a line of blood across Ilara's elegant cheek: a scratch caused by flying shrapnel.

"Uh, Ilara—your cheek . . ."

Ilara put her fingers to the scratch. They came away bloody. She stared at the red on her fingertips, and her cat eyes narrowed.

"Right, then," she snarled, and she stormed out past them into the passageway.

The Mechanics were so surprised at the sight of her walking boldly into their line of fire that at first they didn't think to actually shoot her. That hesitation proved to be decisive. With an angry cry, she threw out her hand and a shock wave blasted up the corridor, denting metal and cracking pipes. When it hit the Mechanics, it blasted them flat against the walls and the ceiling as if they had been swatted by a giant hand.

After the shock wave passed, nobody was firing any-more. There was a long sucking noise as one of the Mechanics unpeeled from the ceiling and landed in a heap on the floor.

Jack and the others surveyed the devastation. Jack swallowed and made a mental note never to give her reason to get angry at him.

"The bridge is this way," she said curtly, and strode off up the passageway, past the bodies of the fallen guards.

. . ✦ . .

The door to the bridge hissed open. Mazzy retracted her data cable from the keypad, and Gradius led them inside, aiming his blaster this way and that. They were relieved and a little surprised to find that nobody was here.

"I guess the whole thing's automatic," said Boston, looking about. "You don't really need a pilot if all you're doing is flying a great big bomb through a rift gate."

"Do you think those guards knew they were on a one-way mission?" Thomas wondered.

"Probably," said Mazzy. "But they didn't care. They're not individuals anymore; they're part of the Kernel."

Boston headed to the controls. A huge viewing window showed a bruise-colored sky. There in the distance, getting larger, was the rift gate, a shimmering hole in the sky sucking in clouds. Boston hit a few buttons but came up with nothing.

"I'm shut out. It's on autopilot."

"I'm on it," said Mazzy, plugging herself into the captain's console. Immediately her eyes began to scroll with data.

Jack's eyes drifted to a screen that showed Earth turning slowly in space, beneath a single word: *Destination*. Nearby, a timer was counting down the minutes to zero.

"Wait . . . it's going to *Earth*?" he cried. "They're going to blow up *Earth*?"

"Sure looks like it," said Mazzy.

"No!" Thomas cried.

Jack just stared, dumbstruck by the unbearable tragedy of seeing his home planet destroyed. All those billions of lives, gone in an instant. All that beauty. Earth hadn't treated him all that well, if he was honest, and nobody else seemed to think much of it; but seeing it there, a cloudy marble in the darkness, it seemed utterly precious.

"The course to the gate is locked in," Mazzy said. "There are firewalls a mile high around everything. By the time I got through, it'd be way too late. And there's a countdown on the bombs in the cargo hold; they're going to detonate a few seconds after the Firehawk passes through the rift gate." She cursed. "They really made sure. I can't stop it."

"But we have to do *something*!" Thomas cried, pointing at the screen. "Who's going to make all the reality shows otherwise?"

"Hey!" called Boston. "We've got company!"

Jack and Gradius hurried back to the door. Striding through the smoke in the corridor, stepping over the fallen Mechanics, was a figure dressed all in black, his face a mirror. He was carrying a sword in one hand that smoked with strange colors, and a blaster in the other.

"Vardis," said Gradius darkly. He drew his own sword from the sheath on his back. It seethed with the same weird energy. "Stand aside. I'll deal with thi—"

He was cut short as the door to the bridge slammed shut in front of him. Jack had his blaster pointed at the keypad mechanism and had blown it to pieces.

"That ought to keep him out for a bit," said Jack.

"Good work, kid," said Boston. "He can't open it if the keypad's ruined."

Gradius gaped at them, aghast. "But . . . I was going to duel him!"

"Duel him later; we're trying to save Earth here," said Jack. "Mazzy? Any ideas?"

"Wait. I think I have one," she said. She pulled out her data cable from the console and began typing frantically. She hit a key to enter the command, and the picture of Earth changed to show a huge white rocky planet instead. She whooped and clapped her hands.

"Arcturus Prime, everybody! The Firehawk's new destination! Where the most it'll destroy is a bunch of dusty old temples."

"And that cute snuffly rabbit hologram we talked to," Thomas pointed out.

"And the Fangbeast, if it's still alive," Jack added.

Mazzy rolled her eyes. "Still, better than seven billion people on Earth, though, right?"

"Totally!" said Jack. "You rock! How did you do it?"

"Well, I couldn't do anything to the Firehawk itself, but I *can* affect the rift gate. So I set it to beam a different destination to the gate, which will send it to . . . er . . ." She trailed off as she saw the picture had switched to Earth again. "Wait, that's not right."

"It's going to Earth again? Change it back!" Thomas urged, jigging anxiously. The rift was looming large in the viewscreen now. The Firehawk was getting close.

"Will do," said Mazzy. She typed in the coordinates for Arcturus Prime once more, and the picture switched back to the tomb world. "There!"

The point of Vardis's sword plunged through the bridge door. As they watched, he began to drag it horizontally, slicing through the metal as if it were fudge.

"He's making himself a door!" Thomas cried.

"That is one sharp sword," Boston said admiringly.

"A vorpal blade," said Gradius. "It will cut through anything."

"The screen has changed back again!" Jack cried, his voice touched with panic. And it had, back to Earth.

Mazzy cursed. "Wait, let me figure it out."

"We don't have time to wait! There's a psycho ninja with some kind of ultimate sword slicing through the door!"

"Hey, it's not *that* ultimate," Gradius said. "I've got one, too!"

"Whatever. Is there a way out of here?"

Dunk harrumphed. "Well, when we were building these things, I seem to remember we put service ducts all over the bridge so we could get to the machinery behind the walls." He lumbered over to a console, tore it from the wall, and tossed it aside. Behind it was a panel, which he tore off as well, revealing a crawl-space. "There you go," he said. "One escape route."

"Wait," said Mazzy. Her face was pale. "We can't escape. Not yet."

"Gonna need a pretty good reason to stop me," Boston said, already heading for the crawlspace.

"Someone has to stay," she said. "Someone has to stay on board till this thing explodes."

They all stared at her. "Explain," Ilara said.

"The Firehawk sends a signal to the rift gate every thirty seconds, updating its destination. That destination is set to Earth. If we switch it to something else, it'll only change back thirty seconds later, the next time the Firehawk talks to the gate. So that means . . ."

"That means that someone has to change the destination less than thirty seconds before the Firehawk enters the rift gate," said Gradius.

"Exactly. And that person is not going to be able to get off."

They were silent as they considered what she had just said. The only sound was the rumble of the Firehawk's engines and the steady fizz of Vardis's vorpal blade as it carved a path through the door.

Gradius scanned the room. "So," he said, "any volunteers?" He looked at Dunk.

"You must be joking," said Dunk.

He looked at Ilara. She just laughed.

"Boston?" he said.

"Nah," said Boston.

"Mazzy?"

"It's not *my* planet," said Mazzy, still working at the console. "I'm sending a signal to the Epsilon right now. I've got the release codes for the dock where they impounded her. She'll be airborne and here in minutes."

"Thomas!" said Gradius, appealing. "You have family on Earth!"

"Yes, I do," said Thomas. "But I'm also a big fat coward, so . . ." He shrugged.

Lastly Gradius turned to Jack and slapped him manfully on the arm. "Jack, Jack, Jack. This is your chance to be a hero, Jack. Your chance to show the world you can amount to something, that you're *better* than just a spare."

Jack took Gradius's hand and peeled it off him. "You know what?" he said. "I learned something, hanging out with these guys. I worked out why I was so bad at all those tests Mom and Dad set me. It's because I don't *need* to be the best. Who'd want all that

275

pressure, all that expectation? There's only space for one up there, and that's a pretty lonely place to be. Sometimes, it's enough just to be on the team." He thought about that for a moment, then added: "Actually, that's where I'd rather be."

Gradius gaped at him. "You mean . . . you *want* to be a loser? That's the worst philosophy I ever heard!"

"Maybe," said Jack. "But I'm not the one who's about to sacrifice their life for the greater good."

Gradius sagged. "It pretty much has to be me, doesn't it? I mean, otherwise I wouldn't be much of a hero."

"Sorry," said Jack.

"I was sort of hoping some expendable sidekick would step up and take the hit out of loyalty. That's how it usually works."

"Yeah, well. Not today."

"Are we going, or what?" Mazzy called, crouching by the service duct. Vardis had almost carved a perfect rectangle out of the door and was about to break through.

Jack studied his more handsome and accomplished double, and for the first time, he felt sorry for him.

Being the best was a heavy responsibility. He was glad it didn't lie on his shoulders.

"Good luck," he said.

"Be safe," Gradius replied. "When I'm gone, it might be you who has to carry the flame, you who will be the new Gradius Clench."

"No offense, but I'd rather not," said Jack. And he hurried off to join the others, leaving Gradius standing there alone, his sword and his blaster in hand.

He really did look like a hero, Jack thought.

The heart of the Firehawk was a dark, clanking maze of metal walkways and stairs. Huge vats seething with strange energies boiled in the gloom, massive pistons flexed and pumped, vents hissed stinking gases, and electricity crackled in the heights.

They came clambering out of a hatch near the floor, Dunk in the lead, and stood there rolling their shoulders to stretch out stiff muscles. It had been a tight crawl through the service ducts from the bridge. Now that they were finally able to stand up again, they didn't much like the look of their surroundings.

"Are you sure this is the way?" asked Thomas doubtfully.

"'Course I'm sure," said Dunk huffily. "Up past the engine takes us to the roof. That's where we want to go, isn't it?"

Mazzy looked like she was listening to something that nobody else could hear. "The Epsilon's close enough that I can pick up her broadcasts now. She's coming in fast. If we can get to the roof, she'll get us off."

"What about the battleships?" Jack asked, remembering the enormous Mechanic aircraft they had seen near the rift gate.

"She can handle those, even with one of her engines out. She'll use the Firehawk as cover. They won't take the risk of hitting it; not with all that antimatter in the cargo hold."

"You think Gradius will be all right?" Thomas wondered, looking back at the hatch they had emerged from.

Jack gave him a look. "You mean, do you think he'll survive being on board the Firehawk when a giant bomb goes off that's big enough to destroy a planet?"

"Oh yeah," said Thomas. "His chances are a bit slim when you put it like that."

"Time's ticking, everyone," said Boston. "Let's get going."

. . ◦ ✦ ◦ . .

It had taken Vardis only a few minutes to cut a long rectangular line through the metal of the bridge door. When the rectangle was complete, the slab of metal tipped forward and crashed to the ground, smoking at the edges. Vardis stepped through the gap, and Gradius opened fire.

Three blaster shots, aimed with perfect accuracy. Vardis's vorpal sword blurred, and the shots deflected away.

"Let's not waste our time with that, shall we?" he said.

Gradius holstered his blaster and readied his sword. Vardis moved closer, ready with his own. Gradius saw himself reflected in that mirror mask. He was calm, cool, composed. Or at least, that was how it looked from the outside.

Vardis leaped, and their swords met. Metal crashed

together in a flurry of blows, now high, now low. Puffs of vorpal energy burst free each time their swords came together, and trailed through the air behind their blades.

They dodged, rolled, and backflipped, stabbed and swung in a deadly dance. Immediately it was clear that Vardis was an expert swordsman, at least as good as Gradius, if not better. Whenever Gradius thought he'd found an opening, Vardis saw it coming and knocked his sword away; whenever Vardis found a gap, Gradius spotted it and parried. At last they broke apart, panting. Neither had scored a hit on the other.

The Firehawk had almost reached the rift gate now. The viewscreen was filling with swirling colors and flashing lightning as they neared. The Mechanic battleships that guarded it had moved away and hung in the air at a distance, making space for the Firehawk to go through. Gradius was aware that time was short, that he had to deal with Vardis quickly, but there was something about his opponent that bothered him. Something *familiar*.

"Who are you?" he demanded. "Take off your mask."

Vardis, his sword still held ready, reached up with one hand and undid the clips holding his mask on. It dropped to the floor at his feet.

For one absurd moment, it seemed as if the mirror was still covering his face. Gradius stared at an exact reflection of himself. Then Vardis smirked, and the illusion was broken. He was a clone, just like Jack was. One of the ten.

"So that's how Kara knew what I looked like," said Gradius. "That's why the first Gradius Clench walked into an ambush and the other clones have been dropping like flies. That's how the Mechanics decoded Jack's distress signal and sent the Hunters to Earth. I should have guessed."

"Yes, you should have," said Vardis. "But you didn't."

"Why did you do it? Why sell us out to the Mechanics?"

"I saw the list," Vardis said.

"The list?"

"We were ranked in order of who was most suitable to be the next Gradius Clench. But I bet you knew that."

"I suspected."

"Well, I saw it," said Vardis, circling closer with his blade ready. "They had us graded. Guess where I was. Sixth! *Sixth!* I was the best fighter of all of us, but they had . . . *questions* about my attitude! Can you believe that? They didn't think I was hero material!"

"You did betray us all and endanger the entire universe," Gradius pointed out.

"That was *afterward!*" he snapped. "You should understand! You were a substitute like me! An understudy! A spare part! If not for me, you'd never even have been Gradius Clench at all!"

"That's true," said Gradius. "But I was happy to wait for my chance. To do my part. We can't all be number one." A faint smile touched his lips. "Sometimes, it's enough just to be on the team."

"Well, you got one thing right," said Vardis. "We can't all be number one. And I've killed every other clone between me and the top. So that just leaves you."

He lunged, and their swords crashed together again.

· · ✦ · ·

Jack and the others hurried onward through the gloom, ears battered by the grinding din of the Firehawk's engines. Dunk led them steadily upward through clouds of steam and thin smoke. Great bolts of electricity snapped and sparked as they jumped between towers, making Jack duck his head instinctively.

"The Epsilon's in place," Mazzy told them. "Waiting for us right above. She says the rift gate's getting awfully close."

"Nearly there," said Dunk, stumping along ahead of her. They were high up, crossing a walkway that passed between two huge tanks. At the other end was a junction where more stairs led to the top of the chamber and out. "It's just over the—"

"Beware!" shouted Ilara, pointing upward.

Her warning was the only thing that saved them. They threw themselves aside as a great jet of flames rolled out of the darkness and licked across the walkway. Thomas tottered away from the fire, shielding his face, and bumped up against the railing. Jack watched with horror as the railing gave way, rusted screws snapping beneath his weight. Thomas tipped backward, flailing, and fell. Jack dived toward him, threw out a hand, and caught him by the wrist, almost wrenching his own arm out of the socket as he did so. Thomas clutched on to him, whimpering in fright, legs kicking empty air. Jack looked desperately for help, but there was none to be found. The others had retreated back up the walkway, Boston clutching a burned hand.

"Jack!" Mazzy cried. "Jack, move it! He's coming!"

Jack tried to haul Thomas up, but he was way too heavy. There was another walkway not far below them. He could let Thomas drop and he wouldn't be hurt. But then Thomas would be down there, alone, and everyone else would be up here.

Thomas could see what he was thinking. He shook his head frantically. Leaving him alone in this place, he'd be good as dead.

Jack looked up the walkway. Black smoke drifted across the junction. Clanking footsteps could be heard coming down the stairs.

Scorch.

He watched in terror as a hulking silhouette emerged from the murk, with a softly glowing dome where a head should have been. Chips of light like evil eyes floated in the gas trapped inside, which flickered with tiny sparks of lightning. In his gloved hands was the nozzle of a flamethrower.

"Jack!" Mazzy shouted again from the other side of the walkway, where they had taken shelter behind one of the tanks. "Run!"

But Jack couldn't run. He was stuck hanging on to Thomas. Scorch raised his flamethrower. Jack began to panic as he realized he had no way to avoid the fire, nowhere to go.

Nowhere but down.

Scorch sent a blast of flames rolling along the walkway toward him. Jack couldn't pull Thomas up, so his only choice was to go over with him. He dug his toes in and pushed himself forward, tipping over the edge. Thomas yelled as the two of them tumbled through the air. Jack felt the burning heat as the flames roared past above him. Then Thomas crashed down onto the walkway below, and Jack landed on top of him, and they both lay there gasping as the fire overhead snuffed out, leaving them singed and bruised but alive.

"I think you broke my ribs," wheezed Thomas. "All of them."

"Well, I think you gave me a hernia," Jack replied. "Get up. Scorch is still after us."

He pulled Thomas to his feet as Scorch walked slowly onto the walkway above, his heavy boots clanking as he neared. There he stopped and tore away the railing with one metal fist. Mazzy and the others began yelling at him, calling him all kinds of names, trying to draw his attention toward them, but Scorch was not going to be distracted. He dropped down to the lower walkway where Jack and Thomas were.

"Why's he after *us*?" Thomas wailed as they took to their heels.

"He's after me," said Jack. "He thinks I'm Gradius."

"Well, that's just great!" Thomas cried. "What's the point of him sacrificing himself if we die, anyway?"

"I'll pass on your disappointment when we meet him in the afterlife," Jack replied.

A few minutes. That was all they had. If they weren't off the Firehawk by then, it would all be over.

Things weren't looking good.

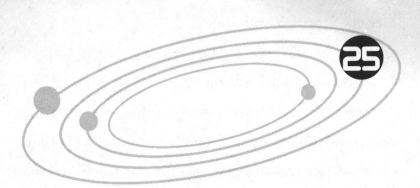

25

Gradius was fighting hard. Harder than he'd ever fought in his life. It didn't make any difference. Vardis was winning.

"While you were training to be a spy, I was training to be a *killer*!" Vardis said through gritted teeth, raining another flurry of blows down on Gradius. Gradius tried to hold his ground, but Vardis was too fierce and he was forced back. In desperation he rolled away and sprang back up onto his feet, only to find Vardis already swinging toward him. He barely blocked it.

Vardis would beat him. It was only a matter of time.

And time was something he didn't have. He glanced over at the countdown. Only a few minutes left, and the rift gate was almost upon them.

"What did she say to you?" he cried as he backed away desperately. "What did Kara promise you in return for selling us out?"

"She persuaded me to be on the winning side. The Mechanics are coming, Gradius. They're taking over the whole Nexus. I won't be a victim."

"You won't be anything if you're dead! Don't you know this aircraft is going to explode?"

Vardis stopped his assault. His eyes narrowed. "What did you say?"

"The cargo hold is stuffed with antimatter! This aircraft is one giant bomb, and it's going to detonate as soon as it gets through the gate! With both of us on it!"

"Kara never said anything about a bomb!"

Gradius saw a chink of hope. "She's using you, Vardis. She just wanted you to keep us busy so we didn't derail the Kernel's plans."

Vardis looked lost. "No . . . She wouldn't!"

Gradius held out a hand. "You can't trust them, Vardis. You're just meat to the Mechanics. Join me, and maybe we can stop all of this."

"Yes . . ." said Vardis. "Yes, you're right. After all, we're like brothers, right?"

"Right," said Gradius.

Vardis's sword flicked out, faster than a snake's tongue. Gradius's blade was sent spinning out of his hand. He drew his blaster, but Vardis was too fast, knocking it away, tripping him to the floor. Gradius landed heavily, with the point of Vardis's sword at his throat.

"You let your guard down, *brother*," said Vardis, with a cruel grin. "Of course I know about the bomb. That's why I had to hurry you along by pretending to believe your sob story. It'll take me less than two minutes to get outside, and I have a parachute. By my count, I have just enough time to kill you and be off this barge before it hits the gate." He grinned. "So let's not waste any more of it. Goodbye."

26

"You think we lost him?" Thomas asked as he hurried with Jack through winding passageways in the depths of the Firehawk.

There was a burst of flames from somewhere behind them, briefly lighting up the dark.

"We didn't lose him," said Jack grimly. He was acutely aware that every passing moment brought them closer to the end, but no matter how they tried, they couldn't get the Hunter off their tail. Jack indicated a doorway. "Down here?"

Thomas shrugged. "Sure. Any way's good when you don't know where you're going."

They stepped out onto a platform and found themselves in a large chamber with a walkway to another platform on the far side. Down below they saw that the bottom of the chamber was covered with dozens of cone-shaped projections. Lightning danced restlessly between them. At either end were large banks of blinking consoles joined by clusters of pipes that stretched along the length of the walls. Chains hung down from above on sliding pulleys, perhaps to lift and replace the cones when they were broken.

"Is that a door on the other side?" Thomas asked, squinting into the gloom.

"Looks like it," said Jack, heading out across the walkway.

Thomas looked nervously over the railing as he followed. Colored lightning snapped and crackled there. "Looks like a power chamber or something," he said.

"Let's just get out of here."

They reached the platform on the other side, but when they tried the door, they found it locked. Jack stared at the keypad in frustration. "Where's Mazzy when you need her?" he asked.

Where *was* she? Probably on the Epsilon by now, with the others. It would be crazy for them to hang around, after all. They'd only known him and Thomas for a few days, and they were only Earthers. He'd been kidding himself really, thinking that he and Thomas were becoming a part of that crew. Still, it saddened him terribly to think that he wouldn't see them again. Especially Mazzy. He'd miss her abuse.

He had other things to worry about now, though. Like getting them off the Firehawk before they were blown to atoms.

"Jack!" Thomas whispered, pulling at his clothes. Thomas was pointing to the doorway. Even over the noise of the engines, they could hear the clank of boots. "Hide!"

They split up and crammed themselves behind the consoles on either side of the platform, where there was just enough space to fit. Jack watched fearfully as Scorch appeared at the doorway of the room, a small flame licking restlessly from the nozzle of his flamethrower. With that door locked, they were trapped.

Scorch stepped into the room, scanning it suspiciously with his alien eyes. Slowly, his hands ready on the flamethrower, he approached along the walkway.

"He's gonna find us!" Thomas hissed frantically, from across the platform. The noise of the engines meant that only Jack could hear him. "Shoot him!"

Jack felt for his blaster, and his heart sank. It was gone. He'd only had it stuffed loosely in his belt, and it must have come free when he and Thomas had fallen off the walkway earlier.

He searched for a plan. If Scorch caught them here, it would be the end. They needed a way to escape. Frantically he cast about for inspiration. The machinery he hid behind provided cover, but only until Scorch got close enough. Unless . . .

Suddenly he had it. "Thomas!" he whispered. "The pipes! Climb along the pipes!"

Thomas saw what he meant. The consoles were joined by a mass of pipes that ran along each end of the chamber, enough to partially hide them. They could climb along them, and if they were lucky, they would remain unseen. If they weren't, they would fall into the crackling power cones below, or Scorch would see them and they would be sitting ducks. But it was the best idea Jack had.

"I can't," said Thomas, shaking his head. His eyes were wide with fear.

"You have to!" Jack said. "You can do it! You're braver than you think!"

"But what if I'm exactly as brave as I think I am? Which is to say, not at all?"

"Just trust me!" Jack hissed in exasperation. "It's our only chance!"

Thomas wavered, uncertain. Jack softened as he realized he was being too harsh. He heard his own words come back to him: *Not everyone is cut out to be an action hero.* Thomas was the kind of kid that gym class was invented to humiliate.

"Hey," he said. "I believe in you."

And that was all it took. Thomas's quivering lip firmed, and he clambered up onto the console and squeezed behind the pipes. Jack climbed up the other side, creeping as quietly as he could through the small spaces. Slowly and carefully they made their way off the platform and out into the chamber.

Scorch prowled down the walkway in one direction. Thomas and Jack crawled along the pipes to either side, heading the other way. If all went well, they could get behind him, slip through the open doorway, and run.

Jack peeped out. Through gaps in the pipes on the other side, he could see Thomas moving. Scorch's attention was fixed straight ahead, and he didn't spot them as they slipped past him.

Keep going. Keep going.

He was so worried about Thomas that he didn't see the chain hanging in his path until he brushed against it. It swung aside, bumping against a pipe with a clank.

Scorch turned toward the sound. Jack crouched down behind the pipes, keeping still. Maybe Scorch wouldn't see him. His heart thumped hard in his chest.

Scorch, suspicious, lifted his flamethrower and aimed it. *He's going to torch this spot, just in case!* Jack thought. Stranded where he was, he could do nothing to avert his fate. Then—

Ponk. Scorch made a quizzical noise and put his hand on top of his domed head. Spinning away into the gloom was an inhaler that had just ricocheted off it. The Hunter turned away from Jack to where Thomas cowered behind the pipes on the other wall, wearing the expression of someone who deeply wished they could take back what they had just done.

Scorch raised his flamethrower again, pointing it at Thomas. Flames tickled the nozzle as his finger reached for the trigger.

Jack had no time to think, only to act. A memory flashed into his head, a memory of his home, and his dad, and that awful assault course that had been the bane of his life. Memories of swinging on a rope across a muddy pit, exhausted arms trembling as he did it again and again.

He looked up at the chain that dangled near him. It hung from a wheeled pulley on the ceiling. *Mom, Dad, this one's for you*, he thought. Then he stood up, grabbed it . . . and jumped with a cry into the air.

Scorch whirled at the sound, alerted too late to Jack's presence. Jack swung across the chamber on the chain, howling with fear and excitement, and planted his boots square into Scorch's armored chest. It was like crashing into a wall, but it was enough to send the Hunter staggering. He hit the railing of the walkway and it buckled beneath his weight. Flailing at the air, he toppled over backward and dropped like a stone, right onto the energy cones beneath.

Jack was already running for his life toward the door by the time Scorch hit bottom and the tank of fuel on his back exploded. Flames billowed up in a dirty cloud. The last thing Jack knew was being lifted up by an invisible force and thrown forward. Then he struck his head and it all went black.

· · ✦ · ·

Gradius lay on the floor and stared up the length of the sword at the clone who would replace him. Desperate ideas flickered through his head, but none of them would work. His sword was on the other side of the Firehawk's bridge; his blaster lay nearer, but out of reach. There was no way in the world he could move fast enough to avoid the blade that hovered at his throat. He was going to die.

Then there was a noise like thunder, an explosion in the guts of the aircraft. A shiver ran through the whole of the Firehawk, and it tilted suddenly. Vardis stumbled backward, off balance. The tip of the sword wavered away from Gradius's throat. Gradius moved without hesitation, seizing at his only chance, kicking Vardis's legs out from under him. As Vardis crashed to the floor, his sword falling from his hand, Gradius was already scrambling to his feet, racing toward his blaster.

He had only a second to act. He dived and shoulder rolled over the blaster, picking it up as he went. He came up facing the other way, back toward Vardis, ready to fire. Vardis, halfway up from the floor, already had his own blaster out and was aiming it.

Two weapons fired at once. Two bolts of energy shrieked through the air.

Vardis gasped, holding his chest. Smoke seeped out from beneath his fingers. His eyes lost their focus and his gaze went far away, and he slumped down on his back.

Gradius picked himself up and walked over to his

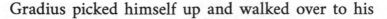

clone, clutching his shoulder where he had been shot. He kicked Vardis's blaster away and looked down at him, his face tight with grief. No matter what he'd done, shooting Vardis had been like shooting his own family.

"I just . . ." Vardis gasped, trying to raise his head. "I just wanted . . . to be . . . number one . . ."

He lay back and said nothing else.

.. ✦ ..

Jack awoke to a painful slap across the jaw. He put a hand to his cheek and glared up at Mazzy.

"Is that the *only* way you know to wake people up?"

She broke into a relieved smile. "We thought you were dead!" she said.

"I thought you'd left us."

"What? And give up the chance to die looking for you? No way!"

Jack lifted himself onto his elbows and saw Thomas being helped into the corridor by Dunk. He was woozy and looked like he'd fallen into a barbecue but otherwise okay.

"What was that explosion?" Mazzy asked.

"WHAT DID YOU SAY?" Thomas bellowed. "I CAN'T HEAR! THERE WAS AN EXPLOSION!"

"It was Scorch," said Jack as Mazzy pulled him to his feet.

"You took out one of the deadliest Hunters in the Nexus?" Ilara asked. She looked dangerously close to being impressed.

"*We* did," said Jack, putting his arm around Thomas. "Don't mess with Earth, right?"

Thomas gave a double thumbs-up and a cheesy grin. Jack was pretty sure he hadn't heard what he said and didn't know what he was agreeing with, but it was nice all the same.

"Can we congratulate each other later?" Boston asked, looking harassed. "Have we all forgotten we're on board a flying bomb?"

"Epsilon's waiting," said Mazzy. "Lead on, Dunk."

They raced through passageways and up stairs. Jack was battered and bruised, but his heart was light and he wore a big grin on his face as he went. Mazzy and the others hadn't abandoned him, after all. Just like he hadn't abandoned Thomas. Just like Thomas hadn't abandoned him. Because that was the kind of thing that friends did.

Real friends. The kind he wouldn't have to leave behind. The kind who wouldn't leave *him* behind.

That's so sweet, I think I'm going to be sick, said Ilara in his head.

Yeah, even you, Ilara, he thought. *You could have run, but you stayed to look for us. So you're my friend, too. Deal with it.*

I'm trying, she thought back, with amused scorn. *It's not easy.*

At last they reached a ladder and a hatch, which Dunk threw open to let in dawn light and rushing wind. They climbed out and onto the roof of the Firehawk, staggering against the flurrying gusts blowing along its hull. The rift gate had almost entirely swallowed the sky, a terrifying hurricane waiting to suck them in.

Nearby, the Epsilon sat with its skids clamped to the hull, her ramp lying open. They stumbled across the surface of the Firehawk toward it. In the distance brooded the Mechanic battleships, but they dared not fire. When they reached the ramp, they hurried inside. Boston was screaming, "Epsilon! Go, go, go!" even before the last of them were halfway up.

"**Retracting ramp,**" the Epsilon informed them calmly.

"Combat Mode! Combat Mode!" Boston yelled.

"**YEEEEE-HAAA!**" the Epsilon screamed, blasting forward so violently that Dunk almost tumbled out of the half-open ramp. Boston and Jack grabbed on to him long enough for the ramp to close, at which point the Epsilon's big thrusters opened up and sent them all skidding along the cargo bay to gather in a heap at the end.

Jack felt a sensation like he was a rubber band being pulled too hard apart. Then the rift gate closed around them, and they were gone.

• • ✦ • •

The rift gate was now so huge in the Firehawk's viewscreen that the edges could no longer be seen. Gradius sat in the pilot's seat and watched the Epsilon disappear into the sucking hole at its center. For an instant, the aircraft seemed to stretch out like putty, becoming impossibly long and thin, and then it disappeared, carrying Jack and the others with it.

Alarms blared and the Firehawk shook as it struggled to keep its course after the explosion. Gradius smiled to himself. He was calm now. They had gotten away, and his own course was set. From memory, he tapped in the coordinates for Arcturus Prime on his console. The DESTINATION screen changed to show a huge white planet floating in space.

On the other side of the cockpit, a small screen crackled into life. General Kara appeared there, standing in front of the brown, smoky landscape of Braxis Prime as she had been before.

"Citizens of the Nexus. I hope you have enjoyed this time of panic, contemplating your imminent destruction, wondering which planet will be the unfortunate subject of our great demonstration of power. Let me ease your minds now. The Mechanics are merciful masters, and they do not like to waste good resources. Therefore our target is the only planet in the Nexus so riddled with disease that even the Kernel does not want it. Witness now the destruction of Earth!"

The broadcast changed to a split screen, with Kara on the left and a live feed of Earth on the right, taken from some distant satellite that the Earthers probably did not even know was there.

Gradius glanced up at the timer counting down to zero. Twenty-three seconds left. The DESTINATION screen flicked back to show Earth as the Firehawk reset its thirty-second cycle. Gradius hunched over the keyboard, ready to type in the coordinates for Arcturus Prime again.

He stopped. He looked over at Kara, smirking on the screen in anticipation of what was to come. And suddenly he was struck by a better idea.

He entered a new set of coordinates. Ten seconds left. He sat back in his seat as the Firehawk hit the rift gate. Everything stretched . . .

. . . and snapped back into place. Outside the view-screen lay a landscape of brown pipes and rusted junk piles, covered by a poisonous haze. Factories sent plumes of flames into the air, and sludgy, toxic rivers oozed. Down there, a million tiny figures worked, half metal and half flesh, picking over the skin of the Kernel.

Braxis Prime. The home of the Mechanics. The *brain* of the Mechanics.

Five seconds left. On the screen, Kara's smug expression faltered as alarms sounded in the background. The human side of her face fell as she looked up into the sky.

"Oh," she said faintly. "That's not supposed to happen."

Gradius, his feet up on the console, gave her a little salute and smiled to himself. It was good to be a hero.

Two seconds left.

One.

"In the wake of the shocking destruction of Braxis Prime, homeworld of the Mechanics, Allied Planet forces have invaded both Rakkan and the mysterious moon where the Firehawk came from. Initial reports say the Mechanics are confused and disorganized without the Kernel to guide them and are offering little resistance. Mystery still surrounds the circumstances that led to the fall of the Mechanics, and it is still unknown who sent the broadcast that alerted the governments of the Nexus to the whereabouts of the Mechanics' secret base, but it is strongly rumored that this was the work of the elusive superspy Gradius Clench."

"I wonder who told them that?" said Jack, looking sideways at Mazzy.

Mazzy whistled innocently.

It was evening on Gallia, and the sun was setting over an ocean that stretched as far as the eye could see. They sat in deck chairs with their backs to the Epsilon, relaxing on a clifftop on a tiny green island, listening to the cries of distant whales and the screech of circling birds. Boston struggled with a flint and tinder, trying to light the campfire, while Ilara watched with barely concealed amusement. Dunk was over by the cliff edge, lobbing boulders at birds.

Mazzy took off her goggles, and the holographic news broadcast, which she had been projecting into the air, disappeared. "Well," she said. "He did it."

"*We* did it," said Jack.

Mazzy nodded to herself. "Yeah. I suppose we did."

Jack watched her for a moment. She seemed far away. "You think you'll ever go back to Rakkan?" he asked.

"I don't know. I don't know if it will ever be the same after what happened." She shifted uneasily in her chair. "How about you? You miss your Guardians?"

"Yeah," said Jack sadly. "It's funny, but . . . no matter how weird they were, and even though they weren't my parents . . . they were my parents. Y'know?"

"I miss my mom," said Thomas, becoming doleful for a moment. Then he brightened. "Wait, no, I don't."

"Really?"

Thomas shrugged. "It's just better out here."

Jack scratched his hair lazily, basking in the last of the day's warmth. "You know, all this started because you brought me a birthday cake," he told Thomas.

"You seemed lonely," Thomas said.

"Wonder if the Ezy-Mart guy knew that cake they were selling you would set off a chain of events that would end up with us taking down an evil empire?"

"Probably not," said Thomas. "They would've charged more."

Jack smiled faintly at that. "We're not those kids anymore," he said.

Thomas nodded. "I guess we're not."

Boston cursed under his breath as he tried once again to strike sparks with a bandaged hand.

"I've decided I'm quite pleased I chose to honor you

with my company, Boston," Ilara told him. "This has been an interesting time, all in all."

"I'm glad we could amuse you for a while, princess," said Boston sarcastically. He threw down the flint, drew his blaster, and fired several times into the campfire until it burst into flames. "There," he said, with his hands on his hips. He looked over at Jack and Thomas. "So what's next for you two?"

"Er . . ." Thomas said.

"I mean, you're not fugitives anymore. There's the whole of the Nexus out there for you. What do you want to do? I can drop you anywhere."

Jack and Thomas looked at each other uncertainly. "*Drop* us?" Jack said.

"Yeah. Like, take you home or something."

Jack was aware that everyone was watching him expectantly, awaiting his reply. "But we *are* home," he said.

Thomas grinned. So did Mazzy. Ilara raised an eyebrow at Boston.

"Well," said Boston. "As it happens, I do have space for a couple of gofers on the Epsilon. The pay is terrible and the company is worse, but thanks to Dunk we have awesome tea. You boys in?"

"You bet!" Thomas cried. He looked at Jack. "Wait, are we in?"

Jack smiled at Boston. "Yeah. We're in."

"Does that mean they get to do all the grunt work from now on?" Dunk called from over near the cliff edge.

"No, that's still you," Boston called back.

Dunk muttered and threw another rock into the sea.

"Now that that's settled," said Boston, brandishing a bunch of toasting forks, "who wants marshmallows?"

They sat by the fire as the sun went down on an alien world, with the sticky-sweet taste of marshmallows in their mouths, and they talked about this and that and things to come. To Jack, who'd never known anything but tests and training and being uprooted over and over, it felt more right than anywhere he'd ever been. Here, with these people, was where he belonged. The thought of that warmed him more than the campfire ever could.

"Hey," said Mazzy. "You know there's a lot of people

out there who know your face. Not to mention that shady Hexagram bunch who cloned you in the first place. What are you going to say if they come looking for the new Gradius Clench?"

Jack put his feet up on a spare deck chair and leaned back with his hands behind his head. "I'll tell them they're mistaken," he said. "I'm not Gradius Clench. I'm Jack." He grinned. "Jack from Earth."

ABOUT THE AUTHOR

Chris Wooding is the author of more than two dozen books, which have been translated into twenty languages, have won awards including the Nestlé Smarties Silver Award and the Bram Stoker Award, and have been shortlisted for the Arthur C. Clarke Award and the CILIP Carnegie Medal. He also writes for TV and film. Visit him at chriswooding.com.